Also by D. S. Lliteras

Jerusalem's Rain

Judas the Gentile

The Thieves of Golgotha

613 West Jefferson

In A Warrior's Romance

In the Heart of Things

Into the Ashes

Half Hidden by Twilight

THE

SILENCE

OF

JOHN

a novel

D.S. LLITERAS

HAMPTON ROADS
PUBLISHING COMPANY, INC.

Jacket design by Marjoram Productions
Jacket photograph by Jonathan Friedman

Hampton Roads Publishing Company, Inc.
1125 Stoney Ridge Road
Charlottesville, VA 22902

434-296-2772
fax: 434-296-5096
e-mail: hrpc@hrpub.com
www.hrpub.com

If you are unable to order this book from your local
bookseller, you may order directly from the publisher.
Call 1-800-766-8009, toll-free.

Library of Congress Cataloging-in-Publication Data

Lliteras, D. S.
  The silence of John : a novel / D. S. Lliteras.
    p. cm.
  Summary: "A novel focused on the experiences of Jesus' women disciples
throughout the crucifixion and after Christ's death. An examination of the
roots of the church's exclusion of women, and the part they played in
early Christianity"--Provided by publisher.
  ISBN 1-57174-410-X (5 x 7 1/2 tc wdj : alk. paper)
  1. Jesus Christ--Fiction. 2. Bible. N.T.--History of Biblical
events--Fiction. 3. Church history--Primitive and early church, ca.
30-600--Fiction. 4. Women in the Bible--Fiction. 5. Christian
women--Fiction. I. Title.
  PS3562.L68S56 2005
  813'.54--dc22

                                                    2004023556

10 9 8 7 6 5 4 3 2 1

Printed on acid-free paper in the United States

Dedicated

to

Karen Van Cleave

Jesus did not die alone. He died in the company of women and in the presence of John's silence. Yet this silence of one brother disciple resounds more loudly than all the lamentations of sister disciples, who loved and followed and took care of Jesus before and after his death. The power of this silence demonstrates and reinforces the cultural exclusion of women: their contributions to a new religious spirit, their loving support during his life, their heartfelt presence at his crucifixion, their tender care after his death, and their believing witness after his resurrection.

Through the Women of Palestine, Lliteras brings to life the love and the sorrow, the loyalty and the sacrifice of sister disciples, who were present before, during, and after Jesus' crucifixion on Golgotha, and who still claim that presence to this day.

Table of Contents

"Talitha cumi. Ephphatha."
("Little girl, arise. Be opened.")

The Rule was that no man
should ever talk with any woman
in public—not even his own wife,
sister, or mother.

—Palestine, B.C.E.

CHAPTER 1

John

He stood within the shadow of the cross. Among women. He was invisible. Among women. He was paralyzed by the emptiness of his Rabbi's eyes.

An old woman placed her right hand upon his left shoulder and startled him. "John. Where are you?"

He trembled.

She lifted her hand from his shoulder. "Our Rabbi is awake. Speak."

John blinked; sorrow disconnected his ground of being. He opened his mouth; terror arrested his ability to talk.

If he could not speak, they could not accuse him. If he remained still, they would not find him.

He shut his eyes and tried to hurl himself from the present, but the past would not allow it. He clenched his teeth and reached for the future, but he heard his Rabbi's voice instead.

"Woman, behold, your son."

John opened his eyes: his Rabbi's mother stepped closer to her son; his Rabbi gathered strength to speak.

"Behold, your Mother."

Increased emotions provoked several women to surround John. Their anxious breaths were suffocating. They urged him to speak.

John raised his trembling arms to demonstrate his unworthiness but unintentionally acted as Jesus' conductor, instead.

"I thirst."

John escaped from the center of the group and stumbled toward a bowl filled with posca. A dirty sponge, half-submerged in the dark vinegar, was impaled with a long stalk that rested diagonally from the bowl to the ground. He grabbed the stalk and raised the acidic sponge to his Master's lips.

John tried to let go of the stalk when a surge of energy suddenly coursed through his body, but the stalk remained attached to his open palm. He was frightened by this magic, confused by this strange sensation.

He collapsed when the surge dissipated. His eyes crossed when he squinted at the dark liquid sky.

Jesus belched.

John rolled onto his stomach and picked up the

foul sponge. He rose to his knees and pressed the sponge to his cracked mouth. The wine burned his throat.

John dropped the sponge as he stood up and raised his arms; he wept. Lightning split the sky and thunder pealed like a penitent ghost; he waited to be struck dead.

Heaven flickered like an injured firefly. Then the sky flashed intensely and illuminated his Master's thorn-pierced head.

Bolts of lightning struck Golgotha's ground and dispersed many spectators, but several clusters of devoted women maintained their positions near his cross.

Women wept and spectators hollered as John beheld his Master's wounded head:

Patches of flesh were torn from Jesus' scalp; patches of scalp hung raggedly from his head. Hair and scalp, blood and dirt were the elements that composed this grotesque image. But mind and matter, fear and loathing were the rudiments that transformed this image into a hideous abstraction.

John lowered his gaze and beat his breast and managed to remain upright despite the storm's ferocity. The wind blew through him and raked his naked soul. John lifted his gaze:

His Master's left foot was nailed lower to the side of the upright stake than his right foot. A square spike was used to pierce the side of the nonload-bearing ankle and anchor the left foot against the splintered wood for the practical purpose of torture. Fecal matter and mud covered the torn-off nails of three toes. The other two were cracked and blackened. The trauma of the large crushed toe and the extreme attitude of the dislocated index toe accentuated the complex injuries that transformed the extremity into a grotesque object. Cuts and scratches, bruises and abrasions, gouges and puncture wounds maimed the top and the bottom, as well as the ankle and the heel, of the left foot.

John wrenched his gaze from the painful sight to seek the darkness of the tempestuous sky, but his Master's deformed left hand caught his attention:

A square spike pierced the wrist and secured the limb to the coarse crossbeam. The ruined fingertips curled inwardly and almost touched the palm near the base of the fingers. Except for the blackened thumb, all the fingernails were torn off with some of the flesh. Blood and dirt obscured some of the injuries, but the mutilation was too dramatic to conceal.

A long rumble of thunder announced the end of the world.

"Say something!" a woman screeched. "Do something!"

John dropped to his knees and embraced the foot of the thick stake. The piercing cold and the savage storm made him shiver like a helpless woodland creature clinging to the gnarled bark of a tree.

He dragged the right side of his face against the stake as he slumped to the ground from the weight of his sorrow. A large splinter tore his cheek and forced his eyes to flutter; he flinched away from the wood. He combed through his beard with his fingers, found the splinter, and yanked it out. He welcomed the pain. He welcomed anything that detracted him from his guilt.

"Save yourself, if you are the King of Israel!" somebody shouted through the din of the storm.

"King, my ass!" one of the other crucified men shouted.

John pressed his hands over his ears and rocked from side to side like a demented penitent, as the crucified thief ranted venomously.

"There's your . . . King . . . a misfit . . . in the company of women . . . a mad prophet . . . ha! . . . cannot help your—"

John wanted to tear out his ears. Mud seeped into his loincloth.

He looked up at his Rabbi and was startled to see love in his half conscious eyes. John sobbed convulsively. He was determined not to abandon Jesus even though he was a cowardly wretch who was unable to speak. His lips trembled.

Was this . . . this love stronger . . . stronger than death?

John held his gaze as lightning assaulted the sky and illuminated his Rabbi's countenance.

This . . . this could not be the end of love.

John rose to his knees and grabbed the bottom of his Rabbi's wooden stake with both hands. Then he released the stake and pressed the palms of his hands against his ears again to stop the sound of crying infants, the sound of sobbing children, the sound of mourning women, and the sound of that tortured criminal.

The ground trembled. He trembled. Rain pelted the top of his head. Lightning illuminated his shame, his impotence, his cowardice. . . .

He banged his forehead against the wood. He banged his forehead repeatedly in order to substitute external pain for internal agony. He banged his head.

Pain. Blood. Darkness.

CHAPTER 2

Ester

John recovered from his self-inflicted blows and glanced at a nearby woman. He was caught despite his furtiveness.

"Do not overplay your silence," said the woman.

He winced.

"You have deceived the hearts of many." She whispered, "Not all."

He recoiled from this . . . this person of no rank or distinction. This mere member of the group. This follower. This . . . this woman.

She leaned toward him. "We are nothing. You are nothing."

John's left eye twitched. The corresponding corner of his tense mouth angled downward.

Her expression hardened. "You cannot hide disgrace. None of us can." She hissed. "Coward. Bastard dog, inferior to any bitch."

John blinked feverishly. Her insult intensified his fear, his resentment, his fury—he struck her across the face with the back of his right hand.

He raised his arm to strike her a second time but saw the dark specter of his arm projecting from the sacred shadow on the ground, caused by the torches that backlighted the cross.

His fingers contracted and his arm retracted like an injured serpent, which disappeared within the silhouette of the crucifixion.

He looked up and sought his Rabbi's reprimand: anything, anything but this guilt, this shame, this silence. He shifted his panic-stricken eyes back to the aggressive woman.

She hissed. Her venom was poisonous. Rain flattened the mantle that covered her thick hair.

John recoiled from her dangerous beauty.

She wore a common tunic: woolen, brown, full length, and tied to her small waist with a cloth belt, which gathered her garment around her slight feminine body. Her belt bore no decorations and her collar was devoid of embroidery; her woolen mantle, which covered her long black hair, was made from the same cloth used to make her tunic. No amount of plainness in dress, however, could disguise her uncommon, mature beauty.

Her small facial features were set upon a skin so silky that a conscious choice was required not to touch her radiance with a curious finger. Her rich brown eyes pierced through everything. Everything. Sorrow distorted her smooth brow.

She stepped toward John.

An older woman stepped toward her. "Ester. Ester. Remember your place."

"My place is here." She regarded John. "Look at him."

"Look at us," said the older woman.

"Don't try to weaken my contempt. Our men have behaved cowardly."

"Not your place to judge. Not your place!"

Ester ignored the older woman, looked at the head of the cross, and tried to hold back her tears. "He showed us that we were equal. That's our place."

"Be careful, Ester. You'll find yourself dodging stones from those who are mean-spirited."

"Let them come. I'll not give up my freedom now."

The older woman sneered. "What freedom?"

"The one our Jesus declared. Remember?" Ester pressed her thoughts into the past. "He said, *'Blessed are the barren, and the wombs that never bore, and breasts that never nursed.'* Bless us for being women. We are not simple bearers of children, children, children. We are women of heart and soul and mind. We are equal to men in the eyes of our Lord."

"Dangerous."

"Shame on you." Ester pointed at John. "Go ahead. Stand near that silent shadow."

"I will not tolerate disrespect."

9

"Look." Ester's eyes widened. "Our Master's presence. Where's your respect for him?" The older woman shrank away. "Your age does not entitle you to anything." She pointed at Jesus. "See? See that? Nothing entitles you to anything."

The older woman's face grew hard. "What kind of rebellion is this?"

"No rebellion. A revolution. Equal to that of our Messiah's."

"Be careful, Ester. I'll . . . I'll not have anything to do with you if you persist in this . . . this—"

"Equality?" Ester scowled. "You're not worthy of his word. Get away. I'll not have anything to do with you."

The older woman withdrew from Ester and joined her small band of sisters. "You'll get what you deserve."

"If that means submitting to a man like John, I'll welcome any punishment."

"God will strike you down!"

"Well, strike somebody. Anybody! But do something." Ester looked for a stone to throw at the older woman. She abandoned her search when she saw a Roman guard stir from his detached demeanor because of her. She pursued a verbal assault instead. "Where is God, now? Asleep?" She peered at the dark, tumultuous sky. "Do something, Lord! Are you asleep? Don't desert us. Don't leave us with childish men!"

"We warn you, Ester!"

Ester leveled her smoldering eyes at the small

band of sisters. "We! My, my. The courage of we is no better than our men's loyalty to our Master. Look." She pointed at John. "Counterfeit loyalty!" She scanned Golgotha to emphasize her search for other male disciples. "Look! Their courage of we is more invisible than that of women!"

"You'll be judged and punished."

"By whom?" Ester shrieked. "Our—your invisibility is greater than God's." She approached the small band of sisters. "Where are you? Show your face again, if you dare."

The frightened sisters rustled like a flock of agitated birds perched on a barren rock.

Ester laughed. "I thought so." She glanced at John. "You coward." She approached him. "Go ahead. Strike me again. Go ahead! I'll not stand by this time. I'll not—"

John surged toward her; Ester flinched. John's madness intensified; the small band of sisters shied.

Ester planted her right foot behind her. "You fake. You fraud." She clenched her right fist and shook it at him. "You . . . you poor imitation of Christ!"

John howled like an injured dog. He turned away from her and bolted toward his Rabbi. He fell to his knees and banged his head against the wood.

Pain. Blood. Darkness.

CHAPTER 3

Dinah

The ground trembled. Rain pelted the back of John's head.

A sudden shock of light. John shuddered.

Had he awakened from a dream?

John straightened his back, pressed his left shoulder against his Rabbi's stake, and peered at a group of women behind him.

He searched for the dream that seemed like reality. Was it? Was it? Was it?

He saw Ester. She appeared disgusted and emotionally exhausted.

He sat on the mud, pressed his back against the wood, and buried his face in his hands. My God, my

God: he didn't want to know. He didn't want to know what he'd become.

"Ha! You're not God enough to strike down a woman!" The harsh contemptuous voice came from one of the thieves who'd been crucified with Jesus.

John felt as if he'd been struck by lightening.

A woman approached the tortured brute. "Then it's . . . it's true. You're still alive. It's true!"

"What! True!" The crucified thief jerked his brutish head from side to side. "You idiot! What is true?"

John stood up. As he approached the crucified thief, the woman stepped in his way.

"Stay where you are," said the woman.

"Dinah?" The crucified brute finally recognized her voice. "Dinah. What? What are you doing here?"

"I couldn't stay away any longer, Azriel. I couldn't, my love." She scowled at John. "Go back to your lunatic."

John was dumbfounded by another woman's aggressiveness.

Ester laughed.

"You heard my woman!" Azriel shouted. "Crawl back to your lunatic! She's more a woman than you'll ever be a man. That's the truth! Ha! A lunatic Master! Ha! With lunatic followers!"

"Azriel. Darling."

"Damn you, woman! I told you not to stand before me if it came to this!"

"I'll not go. I'll not go, my love."

Azriel's will faltered. Her affection reduced him. "Damn you, damn you, damn you."

The tempest's ferocity grew and threatened to destroy everything beneath it. Two of the Roman guards cowered. Some spectators ran. Many sister disciples knelt on the ground as if it were the end of the world.

John approached the foot of Jesus' cross and dropped to his knees.

CHAPTER 4

Mary

Ester laughed, then turned away from John. She did not want him to see her tears because she did not want to tell him that she understood his fear and helplessness. She refused to explain what it meant to be a prisoner of your body and a prisoner of your thoughts because shared thoughts by an invisible woman was not possible with any man. Damn them.

Lightning cut across the storm-possessed sky and slashed the darkness.

The strobing forces above stimulated Ester's defiance. She scrutinized John's drenched and pitiful figure. "Damn him." She wiped away her tears with the back of her right hand. Anger replaced her moment of weakness toward this . . . this fellow disciple, whose wife was sympathetic to her world view.

Mara and Salome, his mother, and . . . and a few others, as well, she thought. They also saw. They also understood what Jesus meant by equality before God. But still, they were women.

She pulled her wet mantle across her mouth to cover her deteriorating expression. She did not want anyone to see her slip from anger into grief.

Invisibility consumed her, now that she understood its true presence; now that her presence had been altered by . . . by, ironically, a man.

She lifted her gaze and rested her heart upon the inert figure nailed upon the cross. Tears streaked down her cheeks again and dissolved into the rain drops that struck her face. Her eyes blinked uncontrollably. Her lips trembled. The woolen mantle felt rough.

Mary of Magdala emerged from the inner circle of mourning women. She approached Ester, who stood on the other side of Jesus' shadow.

Mary appeared weighted by the wetness of her brown woolen tunic, which adhered to her like a clay mold and revealed her shapely figure. Her mantle drooped down both sides of her rain spattered face and emphasized her forlorn countenance.

Ester took a single step toward her. "Where have you been?"

Mary's eyes were calm. Sorrowful. Mildly disconnected. "With Blessed Mother."

"How is she?" Ester glanced at Jesus. "She must be brokenhearted."

"This is the will of God."

"Are those her words?"

"Yes."

Ester dropped the mantle from her face, then peered at John with contempt. "Look at him. The pitiful creature. His guilt originates from his cowardice before Jesus, as well as from his jealousy toward you."

"Ester, please."

"Don't defend him."

"My affection for John does not diminish my devotion to Jesus."

"He does not share your kind of affection."

"John is devoted to our Master." Mary cast a loving glance at Jesus. "And anyone who is devoted to him must share their affection to all."

Ester pursed her lips. "You truly follow him."

"As John does."

Ester grimaced. "John accompanies him. He does not understand him."

"But . . . but that's why Jesus is our teacher."

"Yes. And John always tries to excel. Jesus sees that."

"Don't be hardhearted, Ester."

"Ahh." Ester stomped on the ground with her right foot. The rain intensified as the wind veered, forcing the drops to travel horizontally like a sand storm, which made Ester shut her eyes and turn away from Mary. She pointed in John's direction with her head bowed. "Look at him. Look. He's no different than that big and clumsy fisherman, who thinks he's more important than . . . than—"

"Yourself?"

Ester raised her head in defiance to the rain and to—, "Mary."

"I'm sorry." Mary meshed her fingers together into a humble fist. "I didn't mean to say that."

"Oh, no." Ester's tone was as hard as stone. "You couldn't avoid seeing Peter or John in my own behavior."

"I'm sorry, Ester. You tongue-tie me. You confuse me. You always have."

"Interesting." Ester stepped within an arms distance of Mary. "Interesting."

"I don't deserve your ridicule."

"No. *No.* You misunderstand me." Ester pointed at John. "He mocks himself. See? He does that at the foot of his cross."

"I think his tears are genuine."

"For himself maybe."

"Ester, you can't see. Even a dog can distinguish a kick from—"

"All right. Keep defending him."

"Jesus does."

The wind intensified. One of the tightfisted groups of women drew closer together. It was hard to understand how they could continue to breathe standing so closely to each other.

Ester turned toward the unwavering stake and crossbeam. Jesus' stillness on the cross entered her heart: his presence was at the center of her world. Ester burst into tears, which rekindled her anger at John, who was slumped against the bottom of the heavy wooden stake. "Damn you." She glared at Mary. "Just because he's the only man among us at our Lord's final hours—well." Ester's scorching eyes supported the tone in her voice. "He shall be labeled a coward." She grimaced. "One can only hope."

"Ester, your cynicism is overwhelming."

"Men make the definitions."

"My God, you are tormenting me."

Ester inhaled to control her temper. She spoke on her exhale. "Then I shall leave."

Mary stepped in her way. "No. Please. Don't leave us."

"Then you must be afraid to be left in John's company."

"You twist everything. Everything."

"I see what I see, Mary. And he stands within our fold like a boy-man. Like an impotent child. What good is that?"

"A man among Roman guards and legionnaires is a helpless being."

Ester shook her head. "Kind. You're always too kind to others. Kinder than they deserve."

"I'd prefer gentle men among us, no matter their degree of strength. John has his capacity."

"Not for gentleness." Ester snickered. "And for truth? Well. He stands among women and pretends. He strikes me and, still, he wins your sympathy—another woman. Let's see how far that will get him in this world. Even a failed man among men carries greater weight than a successful man among women."

Mary unclasped her hands and lowered her arms to her side. "Ester."

The uncovered face of the older woman, who had challenged Ester earlier, emerged from a cluster of brown mantles. The severity of her expression had not changed. When Ester sneered at her, the older woman covered the lower portion of her face with her mantle, turned her head, and disappeared within the cluster of brown mantles again.

"Ask Peter, if you can find him." Ester's lips trembled. She surveyed a nearby group of women and saw Peter's wife, Mara, whose stern face flattened with humiliation. She turned to Mary. "Ask John, if he can speak." She gazed at Jesus. "It's too late to ask our Master." She realized she revealed her own spiritual ambition. She bowed her head in shame. "Why? Why am I so small?"

Mary smiled compassionately. "We all want to be first in line. Don't you know that?"

"Truly? Truly."

Mary referred to John. "His ambition simply . . . simply prevents him from looking around him. Like Peter, he does not notice anyone but himself. He does not feel anything but his own suffering." She nodded at John's fragile figure. "You see?"

"But our Master smiled at him often."

"Our Jesus smiled at all of us."

Ester conceded. "Yes. Yes." She shook her head. "My God, my God, I'm such a wrong-doer. And look at you, Mary. Filled with forgiveness, as it should be. But not me. I'm filled with venom and anger and—oh,

I'm not worthy to be standing near what's left of his shadow."

A blinding bolt of lightning harassed the barren sky, illuminated the surrounding landscape, and intensified Golgotha's shadows. A cluster of sister disciples moved away like a well-trained Roman cohort.

Ester knelt before Jesus. She realized that by judging John, she had uncovered a guilt equal to John's.

"Do not feel ashamed."

"I won't," Ester lied, then glanced at John's pathetic figure clinging to the foot of Jesus' cross. She felt alone and weak and guilty about the jealousy and rivalry with John and Peter over Mary of Magdala's approval and, most of all, over their Lord Jesus' love. Ester laughed insanely.

Mary stepped toward her. "Are you all right?"

"Jesus."

"Yes?"

"He had enough love for us all."

"Are you all right?"

"Yes. Yes." Ester pressed her lips together to prevent tears. "You've known that all along."

"I . . . I think so."

"And . . . and . . ." Ester glanced at John. "There was never any privacy between you."

"His wanting me came as an accident." Gravely. "He's a married man. His wife is our sister. I believe his intentions were honorable from the beginning."

"And in the end?"

"Look at him."

"He . . . he wanted you," said Ester.

"Because Jesus possessed me."

"And, because John is a man."

"Jesus possessed all of us, Ester."

"I don't care. Men rule. Men. We . . . we must respond to their whims." She stood up and hollered at John. "What is your whim now? Why don't you consult with Peter? Yes. What must we—no. What must I defend myself from now?"

"Be careful, Ester. Be fair."

"Fair! What's fair? What. What is truth?"

"I'm not smart enough to answer you, Ester." She peered at Jesus. "His love goes beyond the capacity of my understanding. I . . . I don't understand. I don't know what I am."

"My God. You're so honest. And you're . . . you're no better than the rest of us."

"Well. Is that so bad?"

Ester closed her eyes as she exhaled. "You humble me."

"I'm sorry."

"My ordinariness torments me." Ester glanced at Jesus. "He . . . he saw this all along. Oh, God. What a fool I am. What a fool I've been."

"We. All of us. Are fools." Mary returned to her inner circle at Blessed Mother's side.

Ester's expression gradually hardened. She muttered to herself. "No, Mary. I can't. I can't be fair." She glanced at John. "He's all that's left of our men." She grimaced. "What good are they without courage and presence and protection? What good are they?"

CHAPTER 5

Daughter

A blinding bolt of lightning cracked the sky and struck the earth. A deafening clap of thunder paralyzed the minds and stopped the hearts of those brave but frightened souls still left on Golgotha.

Ester stumbled into His influence by stepping onto his shadow. Her spirit crumbled.

She fell to her knees, stripped of her will, her energy, her life's force. Her consciousness gave way to the past made present by her Master's dark outline.

"Yes, I touched you first. Yes, I thought I was breaking the Law. I, an unclean woman, who dared to seek a cure by your touch. I thought I was a wrongdoer. But you didn't consider my uncleanliness. You considered me. Me. A woman who was not to be judged but freed by the touch of your love and encouraged to follow you forevermore." Ester steadied her gaze upon Jesus' empty and battered expression. "Yes, I touched you first. But you chose me, my Lord. My discipleship was . . . was your sovereign decision. You chose me. You chose me."

Pain seized her abdomen. Her breasts still ached.

She had been emotionally premenstrual for several days before her flow. She'd been afraid. The intensity of her cramps had worried her—the pain felt different.

Her bleeding had returned because it was her time. Her thoughts frightened her:

Would regularity give way to irregularity or worse—give way to constant bleeding again? Would his death erase her cure? Jesus. Oh Jesus.

Ester bent forward and pressed the top of her head against the shadow on the ground. Her vaginal flow ceased.

Like the touch of his robe, she felt the change in her body. The threat of relapse into illness again had been thwarted. The threat and its fear had disappeared within the faith of the past made present again. She recalled the incident:

"Who touched my cloak?" Jesus inquired.

Ester trembled.

"You mean to say," Peter asked, from among the other disciples present, "with all these surrounding people pressing against us, you are concerned about someone's touch?"

Jesus ignored Peter. He surveyed those who were nearest him. He sought their eyes.

She was frightened. She knew he was going to discover her. She knew she needed to identify herself. She fell before him and surrendered to his midday shadow, afraid to look into his eyes.

He reached for her chin and directed her gaze to him.

She spoke rapidly, childishly, seriously. "My Lord, for twelve years I have bled constantly. I have suffered greatly in the hands of numerous doctors. They have cost me everything, and they have done nothing for me. In fact, their cures have made me worse. My private pain and constant blood flow have separated me from my people, whom I no longer care about, since they have judged me for no good reason. I've done nothing wrong. Nothing."

"Yet, you've been hurt. Violated."

Ester was startled. "Lord. Nobody knows that but . . . but, Lord, I'm frightened."

"Rest, my daughter. No one else will hear you."

Ester studied the surrounding people. She felt invisible. "Yes, Lord. I was violated by my mother's brother when I was a child of eight. I . . . I did not understand what had happened. I only understood pain and fear and—and I bit the hand he used to cover my mouth. That's all I could do against him." Tears streamed from her eyes. "He left me stunned and irreparably damaged inside. He left me in disgrace forever after, even though this violent act against me cost him his life soon after my mother discovered the blood that soaked through my tunic." Her eyes hardened. "My father's act of justice was swift. But my mother's dark judgment against me left me confused and insecure and resentful. I have hated her and the world." Her eyes softened. "Until now, my Lord. Until . . . until . . ."

Jesus smiled. A long silence passed between them. *"Daughter, your faith has cured you. Your trust has freed you. Go in peace. Say farewell to your past, and to your troubles."*

She raised her head from the shadow of the ground and looked up at her crucified Jesus:

She felt the permanence of his cure. She knew this was not magic. She hoped he would return from the dead. He said. He said.

She cried. She remembered the private things he had told her and the others who followed him from Galilee. She prayed.

CHAPTER 6

Tamar

She stood alone. Battered. Tired. Scarred by deprivation. She did not tremble from the elements but from the suffering caused by her grief.

Her threadbare tunic was mended so often that the garment was a patchwork of old and new and dissimilar wool—every sewn seam could be seen, and permanent stains spotted the beige fabric. Her mantle was so thin with wear and repair that it provided little protection from the weather.

She rarely covered her face. She rarely regarded men's talk. Only Jesus; a little shade, only from Jesus.

Her nose was round and blunt, her skin was brown, and her eyes were deep and dark and raw from the exhaustion of weeping. Her black hair was thick and long and partially braided. Her eyebrows were heavy and almost connected above the bridge of her nose.

She extended her arm in a gesture to attract Ester's attention.

Lightning and thunder and ground movement. The cries of those too frightened to save themselves.

Her gesture dissolved into the surrounding tempest, as well as into the frantic activity of those trying to escape Golgotha and those trying to seek refuge from the weather. "Ester."

"Yes."

"Ester."

"Yes!"

"You do not stand alone."

"I do not stand at all." Ester raised her bowed head. She felt other than human since she was on her hands and knees. "Who are you?"

"A wrong-doer. A woman saved by the scratchings on the ground, and by the words of a single question."

Ester sat back on her feet. "I don't know you."

"That's because I have followed our Master from afar."

Ester wiped her muddy hands on her wet tunic. "We all do."

"No. No. Physically from afar. I . . . I am not worthy to be a known disciple."

"Not worthy. Hmm. Those humble words deceive you. They . . . they make me want to know more about who—who are you?" The wind veered. Her eyes hurt. She adjusted her mantle as she turned away from the angle of the rain. "How do you know my name?"

"I followed you and your sisters from afar. But I managed to listen closely. News travels fast and easy by mouth. You know that."

"All right. So you know my name. Who are you?"

"I . . . I was presented to our Master."

"There have been many people presented to our . . . our Master—Jesus. Many."

"Not at the Temple Courts. And not by the Pharisees. You weren't there."

"Oh. Then you're . . . you're—"

"Tamar."

"Ahh. Yes. I've heard of you." Ester straightened her back. "You're right. News does travel easily when it . . . it means the suffering of a woman."

"An adulteress, you mean."

"No. You're not any longer."

Tamar leveled her proud gaze at Ester. "I remain accused."

"True. But the stain of your wrong-doing is no longer upon your soul."

Tamar exhaled. "Only upon the hardhearted men of Palestine, who do not forgive."

"Men. They are the worst in us." Ester peered at Jesus. "And the best." She lowered her eyes. "Men. They push and pull and force their wills upon us, then slink away while they point their crooked fingers at us." Ester scratched something on the muddy ground, then cocked her head to the side as if she were attempting to decipher what she'd written. "On that day, when you stood accused of being with a man who wasn't your husband, what did he write on the ground?"

"I . . . I don't know. I . . . I can't read. Can you?"

"Some."

"Taught by a good husband?"

"No. By my regretful Father. I've never been married."

"I see. Neither have I."

"Hmm. The man they found in bed with you: was he brought before the enforcers of the Laws of Moses? Was he?"

"What do you think?" Horizontal cynicism cracked the lower part of Tamar's expression without showing her teeth. "The scoundrel slithered away like an uncircumcised snake as they dragged me out of my bed, paraded me through the streets, and brought me before . . . before men of God." Tamar spat on the ground to cleanse herself of her last four words.

"Yes. Men of God. I have spat on the ground many times."

Tamar glared at a small group of women nearby. "What are you looking at!?" Two of the women turned away. One bowed her head. The others expressed disdain. "You. And you. Had Jesus not spoken for me, you, and you would have hurled the first stones."

"You recognize them?"

"Not them exactly, no. But they were there. All of their kind." The disdainful ones dissolved within the huddle. "Why aren't you stoning me now?"

"Because they're cowards."

Tamar approached Ester and whispered to establish an intimacy between them. "'*Rabbi, this woman was found in bed with a man who wasn't her husband. The Law states she should be stoned to death. What do you think?*'" Tamar glanced at Jesus on the wood, then bowed her head in recollection. "I swear he looked among them as if he were looking for someone else. It seemed that he looked behind me as if expecting to find someone standing with me. To my surprise, I wondered: Did it matter to him that no man had been accused? Was I seeing something imagined? Could he have been looking for the other half of adultery? The other half of the Law? What. What? The Pharisees insisted that he answer them. '*What do you think?*' one of them repeated." Tamar's eyes intensified. "Think. Think, I thought. Men asking another man to decide my fate. Me. A woman. A nobody. A nothing. What kind of a dark joke was this? I . . . I can't remember if it was fear or anger that kept me silent. I do remember that shock and amazement was what kept me silent when our Lord simply bent over and started writing on the ground with his finger."

Ester studied her own scratchings in the mud. "I'd give anything to find out what he wrote." The earth trembled.

"You. And me." Distant thunder surrounded them.

"Why didn't you ask him?" The wind changed directions. "Why didn't you?" Lightning split the sky.

Both women cowered.

"In . . . in his presence, I . . . I never felt the need to . . . to—"

"I know." Ester stood up. "I know. His presence had the same effect on me."

"Always. Always. It's only now that many questions arise. Now is the time that I want answers. Now is the time—" Tamar sighed deeply. "His unconscious silence is deafening. I feel hopeless and lonely and broken. Besides, he never answered their question. Why would he answer mine? Why? Without him, I could have thrown the first stone at somebody else. I . . . I hate myself for having to admit this." Grudging tears rolled down her cheeks. "I'm a wrong-doer. And without the light of his presence, I could have picked up a stone and thrown it at a wrong-doer equal to me."

"I understand that kind of anger."

Tamar was astonished. "You. You mean that?"

"I'm a nobody. I'm an outcast as well. My constant menstruation nearly cast me among the lepers. Without his presence, his light, I would have continued to hate and resent all who inhabit this world." She sighed. "I could have picked up a stone."

Tamar struggled to hold back her tears. "Thank you for saying that."

Ester adjusted her mantle. "So. Our Lord Jesus stooped over and scratched words into the ground."

"It looked like words. Then he said; *'Any of you here who have never sinned, go ahead and throw the first stone at this woman.'*" A single tear streaked down Tamar's right cheek. "He did not wait for anybody's response. He squatted by the scratchings he made on the ground, and scratched more letters into the sand with his fingers. To my dismay, nobody protested. To my shock, one of them left. Then another and another until . . . until he and I were there alone. I didn't know whether to shout for joy or to tremble with anticipation. My inclination was to expect violence against me. I flinched when Jesus stood up. As far as I was concerned, he was still a man like any other man."

Ester approached Tamar and touched her shoulder. "And yet, he is not a man—like any other."

"*'Woman, where is everybody?'* he asked, as if he didn't know. As if I could answer him correctly. *'Isn't there anyone left to condemn you?'* What could I say? I was accused. I was. I was one breath away from condemnation and, therefore, death. I . . . I simply said, *'No, sir.'*" Tamar released a long and empty wail, then allowed Ester to guide her tearful face to her sympathetic bosom. "He saved me. And all I could say was, 'No, sir.'"

"There, there." Ester stroked the back of Tamar's head. "He understood your gratitude."

Tamar stifled her tears, then sniffled. She wiped her nose with her left sleeve. "He said. He said, *'I'll not condemn you either. Go your way. Leave your life of sin.'*" She lifted her head from Ester's bosom. "*'Go your way,'* he said. As if, now, there was any other way in my life but his." She hugged Ester. "*'Go your way.'*"

Ester whispered. "I know. I know."

CHAPTER 7

Sisters

The rain's intensity increased.

Ester and Tamar clung to each other:

Sculptured wrong-doers. Paralyzed phantoms. Devoted women. A grieving statue.

Their woolen tunics made vertical contact from breasts to hems; their soaked garments were stretched so taut by the weight of the water, that they appeared to be encased in a brown shell.

The roll of thunder from above accompanied the quaking from below; heaven and earth were acting as one.

A foreign woman emerged from the outer darkness that surrounded Golgotha. She adjusted her mantle several times in response to her self-consciousness, then stepped further into the light.

The timid woman arced widely around the grieving statue. Sidestepped Dinah. Snatched a frightened glance at Azriel. Stole a sorrowful glance at heaven. Then bowed her head to Jesus as if she were immersed in prayer.

The woman was tall, full-figured, and barefoot. Her poverty was carefully concealed by the meticulous care of her overly repaired garments. Her tunic was pulled tightly to her waist by a brown woolen belt tied into place with a simple knot. The dark red and brown vertical stripes of her outer tunic partially camouflaged the frequency of her garment's repair.

Dark eyes. Dark complexion. Full mouth. Prominent nose. Proud and steady composure. Of mixed Samaritan heritage. Yet, all Semitic.

Her long black hair was concealed under her long brown mantle.

"What are you doing here?" a short, stout woman demanded.

The tall woman turned to the small woman and shared her resentment. "The Assyrians conquered your people a long time ago. Not us."

"There was no hatred behind my question," the small woman countered defensively.

"There's hatred in your people over who I am."

"Well. Your people did settle here during our exile."

"Where were we to go? Why not in Jerusalem? You were a captive people."

The stout woman sneered. "Assyrians."

"I have no affection for them either. They wronged both our people. And yet, it is you and I, a Jew and a Samaritan, who hate each other."

"I . . . I don't hate you."

"Hmm."

"I'm Ephah," said the short Jewish woman.

"And I'm Abatal," said the tall Samaritan woman. She studied Ephah. "We are both a twice conquered people. And both our places of sacrifice, Mount Gerizem and Jerusalem, have been desecrated."

"Yes. And the one God is—"

"One God, your God, what God!? You idiots! Who cares?!" Both women cowered from the loud and brutish man who'd been crucified with Jesus.

"Azriel, please," said Dinah. "These women are—"

"Idiots! They're tormenting me with their damn chatter, chatter, chatter!"

"Azriel, my love, please, please." Dinah's beauty increased with her concern for Azriel's torment and pain and approaching death. Her eyes sparkled like diamonds, her uncovered head revealed long hair so black that it shimmered near dark blue. The mantle around her neck partially covered her embroidered collar, which called attention to her success as a tavern keeper; she also ran a successful underground brothel, gambling den, and safe house for those on the run from Rome, Herod, and the Law in general. Her free spirit was her greatest asset. Only a man like Azriel, secure in his masculinity, was able to withstand the diamond-cutting strength of her character, which Azriel sometimes neutralized by his indifferent brutishness toward her.

Azriel exhaled, then lost consciousness.

Dinah bowed her head and clenched her fists in despair.

Ephah whispered. "Like I said, I don't hate you."

Abatal peeked at Azriel as she addressed Ephah. "You neither consider me pure, nor ritually clean. What kind of people encourages that?"

"We. Yes. I have my faults. I'm sorry."

"No. I'm sorry. I, and my people, are no different." Abatal regarded Jesus. "But this man was different."

"My Rabbi. My Messiah."

Azriel groaned. Dinah wept.

"Our Master. The Annointed." Abatal beckoned Ephah to approach her in order to increase their distance from Azriel and Dinah. "He saw me as a woman," she whispered vehemently. "Nothing more. I was present before him. He drank water from my cup. My cup."

"Hmm. And it was a Samaritan who thanked him for healing his leprosy. None of my people did." Ephah exhaled. "Ungrateful."

"You mean, spoiled."

"I don't understand."

"You have the arrogance of Yahweh in Jerusalem."

"I'm . . . I'm sorry."

Abatal looked at Jesus. The rain forced her to blink. "'I am, He,' he said, when I was with him. Alone. One afternoon."

"When?"

"When he was thirsty."

"Who are you, Samaritan?" Ephah demanded.

"One who knows," said Abatal.

"Share this with me."

Abatal stared at the raindrops hitting the muddy ground. "He came through Sychar on his way to Galilee from Judea."

"Hmm. Why else would he pass through Samaria?"

"You need to listen to his words more carefully. He wasn't that way. What kind of disciple are you?"

Shame distorted Ephah's mouth. "You humble me. As you can see, I'm still burdened with the bad habit of prejudice."

"I'm sorry. I did not mean to cause—"

"My embarrassment is my fault," Ephah muttered. "Please. Tell me more."

Abatal whispered to avoid aggravating Azriel or Dinah. "He was sitting at the edge of the well when I came for water at noon." She studied Ephah, who awaited the unfolding of her story. "He asked me for a drink of water as I lowered my bucket into the well."

"Where were the others? There must have been others with him."

"True. But they had gone into town to buy food and drink."

"You mean, all his accompanying disciples had abandoned him? Impossible."

"He was not abandoned," said Abatal. "He is never abandoned." She recollected: "*'Give me a drink,'* he said. *'You're a Judean,'* I said, even though he sounded like a Galilean to me. *'How can you ask me, a Samaritan woman, for a drink of water?'"*

"Why did you address him as a Judean?"

Abatal shrugged. "Jacob's well is on that side of town."

"I see."

Abatal smirked. "I know. I know. Judeans—or Galileans—do not associate with Samaritans."

"I did not imply anything!"

"What's that?!" Azriel's head bobbed several times. "Damn women! Don't you know your place?! Disappear, damn you! Disappear!"

It was hard to understand how words could come out of a crevice so dry and tormented. Azriel's lips were cracked so deeply that his flesh looked like teeth.

Azriel's tortured body writhed; he broke several of his blood clots. His muscular body had been reduced to a pitiful mass of abused flesh nailed to a stake and crossbeam. Nothing could save him: the world had rejected him for the criminal that he was, and he had rejected the one who had offered him his everlasting spirit—whatever that was.

"Azriel, darling. Those women grieve as I do."

"Damn you, woman! I told you to keep your tears to yourself. Can't you see? Men are dying here!" Pain coursed through his body and punished him for the intensity of his anger. "My young partner in crime is a fool! This other idiot is . . . is mad!" He coughed up a dark clump of blood. Choked. Spat. Then laughed bitterly. "And I'm an unlucky thief."

"Darling, sweet darling."

"Don't darling me! I told you not to come here! I told you to stay away if it should come to this!"

Dinah glared at Ephah. "Shut up, damn you!" She frowned at Abatal. "Both of you." Her eyes softened. "Please. Please!"

Azriel gurgled loudly, then passed out.

Ephah waited for Dinah to direct her attention back to Azriel before she whispered. "I did not imply anything. I swear."

Abatal turned away from Ephah. She lifted her gaze, flinched from the raindrops hitting her eyes, then spoke to Jesus. "'How can you ask a Samaritan woman for a drink?' I asked. And he said, 'If you knew the gift of God and who just asked you to give him a drink, you would ask him for a drink instead.' There was no pretense in his eyes. And no concern about his own thirst. He leaned back and supported himself with outstretched arms, since he was sitting on the ground, and said, 'He would give you life-flowing, eternal water.'" She smiled. "He was amusing himself, I thought. So, I said, 'Mister, you have nothing to draw this water with. The well is very deep.'" Abatal winked at Ephah. "Knowing that there was no flowing water from this well, I decided to amuse myself." She grinned. "We were alone. So I continued to flirt with him."

Ephah was shocked. "Abatal."

"What? He was flirting with me, too."

"Not my . . . my, our Master."

"He is a man, isn't he?" Abatal was amused by

Ephah's naiveté. "You don't have to protect his reputation."

"There's nothing to protect. Just look." Ephah stepped into the shadow of the right crossbeam. "What reputation does he have left?"

"His unjust crucifixion does not alter his standing with me. And, I feel sure, the many who believe in him feel the same."

"And this belief. What do you believe of him?"

"I believe he is more than a mere man."

"But as you said, he is a man, isn't he?"

"Yes. But what a man." Abatal knew she had Ephah's full attention, and proceeded with her story about her private moment with Jesus. "'Where will you get this life-giving, eternal water? Can you do better than our father Jacob? He left us this well. He and his family and his cattle drank from it.' Then I wondered if he meant that Jacob's well was actually a water source, not simply a deep shaft. Hmm. I thought, maybe he wasn't being flirtatious after all." Abatal enjoyed the moment of suspense that produced disorder within the Jewish woman's certainty about her Master—whatever that certainty was. Abatal chuckled. "Nah. He was not speaking only of well water. He meant more than that, I think." She noted Ephah's exhale of relief. "He also knew how to flirt as well." Abatal enjoyed teasing Ephah. "And yet, and yet—his words were deep. Very deep. But his tone was plain and reaching when he said, 'Everyone who drinks this water will get thirsty again. But all who drink the water that I give them will never get *thirsty again. This water I give will become a spring of water within them, a source of eternal life.'* My God, I thought, he was no longer flirting. He spoke like a prophet. More. I don't know. His eyes. They changed, yet again." Abatal shook her head. "I don't know what I was asking for, but I asked him for it anyway. I couldn't help myself. I said, *'Mister, give me a little of this water, so I'll never get thirsty or have to keep coming back here to draw water.'* I liked him."

"Our Master was friendly," Ephah conceded.

"Yes. I did not fear his playfulness as I would have with most men."

"All other men, if you ask me."

"See? You agree. I would have suspected any other man of impure intent if they would have said, as he said, *'Go, call your husband and come back here,'* as if he were probing my willingness to be with him. But that wasn't what he was doing. Somehow, I knew that. Somehow, I wasn't afraid to admit to him, *'I have no husband.'* Somehow, I felt transparent to him."

"I don't understand."

"I didn't either." Abatal shrugged her shoulders. "I still don't." She bit her lower lip. Her eyes focused inwardly. "He said, *'You're honest to say that you have no husband. Because you have had five husbands, and the man you are now with is not your husband. You've told the truth.'"* Abatal noticed Ephah taking a step away from her. "Yes. Unclean."

"I didn't mean to . . . to step away from you."

"Hmm. Perhaps. Perhaps not."

"I swear. I meant nothing by that move." Ephah stepped closer to Abatal in order to prove herself. Her lips trembled. Her hands wrung the breast of her tunic. Rain did not cleanse the moment.

Abatal nodded. "'You've told the truth.' That's what he said. How did he know? I thought. How did he know? And I said, 'Master—'"

"Master? Already with Master at this point?"

"Yes. To my own astonishment, as well." Abatal studied Jesus' torn scalp. "Like I said, 'Master. Master, I can see that you must be a prophet. Our people have always worshipped on this mountain. And yet, your people insist that Jerusalem is the only place where anybody ought to worship.'" Abatal lowered her gaze to the foot of the cross. "He remained silent in the manner that encouraged me to reveal myself." She shrugged her shoulders. "Not that I care a fig about worshipping on Mount Gerizim. Five husbands and, now, an unreliable man regularly enjoying my intimacy at night certainly proves that." She grimaced. "Men. Always men and their Gods and their places of burnt sacrifices. Aghh. May a prophet greater than Moses appear." She realized what she said. "Hmm." She looked at Jesus. "Interesting how an expression will persist even after . . . after he told me, 'Woman, believe me, the hour is coming when you won't worship the Father either on this mountain or in Jerusalem. Your people worship what they don't know. We worship what we know. We Jews are the instrument of salvation,' and all that. 'But the hour is coming. In fact, it's already *here. The true worshippers will worship the Father in spirit and in truth, without concern as to place. These are the kind of worshippers the Father is looking for. God is not tied to place. God is spirit. And in truth, those who worship God must only worship him in spirit.'* She sighed. "Those were a lot of words with deep meaning. Beyond my capacity, I thought at the time. Somehow he compelled me to look inward and to speak. I had nothing new to say. All I have are Samaritan beliefs. So I said to him, *'All I know is that the Messiah, the one called the Anointed, is coming someday. And when he does, he'll show us every-thing.'* I was surprised by his response. I should have been terrified, but I wasn't."

Ephah took hold of Abatal's right hand. "What did he say?"

"He said, *'You've been speaking to the Anointed all along.'* " She whispered. " *'I am, He.'* "

Ephah peered at Jesus. "Yes. The Messiah."

"I am. I am. I wanted to be frightened in his pres-ence, but I wasn't. I wasn't!"

The ground trembled as if the soul of God had grumbled. Both women tried to conceal their fear. But a dangerous arc of lightning streaked the heavens and illuminated the terror-filled expressions etched deeply upon their faces before continuous thunder almost loosened their bowels.

Abatal was determined not to be vanquished by her fear. She reached for the lower portion of her mantle with her left hand in an unconscious effort to cover her face. She raised the wet wool to her chin, but she did not conceal her mouth. "I wasn't frightened. Not until his followers returned. A ragged lot. Hateful, if you ask me."

"I *am* asking you."

"Well. It's not what they said. It's what I saw in their eyes, and in their restrained expressions." Abatal snickered. "Their Master had them trained—no. No, that's not fair to him. Even he can't stop the pettiness among us. Even he can't fully wipe away the prejudice that exists between our people." Exasperation distorted her countenance. "The biggest one of the lot stepped between us and glared at me with eyes that said I didn't belong with him; what was I doing talking to him?" She chuckled. "He dared not ask openly: What was Jesus doing talking to me?" She adjusted her mantle to dramatize her resentment. "I wasn't doing anything indecent with this man."

"You know the Law," Ephah countered. "A woman is not safe from scrutiny, especially in a public place."

"Yes. I could see the envious puzzlement, the resentment, even the stone throwing potential in their eyes." Abatal studied Jesus. "What has his crucifixion accomplished? I still see fear. Feel emptiness. Even now, both conditions are what's left on his face. Fear and emptiness remain with us all. From that there's no escape: in life, in death, in childbirth, and in the presence of those who love you, and hate you."

"That's the first sensible thing I've heard either

one of you say," said Dinah, hardened by the torture
that her man was enduring. She remained bareheaded
in defiance to the weather, to the world, and to her
own weariness.

"And who asked you for your approval?" Abatal
challenged.

"Abatal!"

"That's right," said Dinah. "You should caution
her." She pointed at her man dying on the cross.
"What you see there is an example of the kind of pain
you'll suffer if you should awaken him into his misery again. He's all I believe in and he'll be gone soon.
Get away from here or I'll . . . I'll . . ."

Ephah pulled Abatal's arm. They shrank away
from this truly pagan woman, who further dismissed
them by attending to her man.

Abatal stared at Jesus' shredded feet. "I ran from
them."

"Who? Oh. Yes," Ephah whispered, as she nervously turned away from Dinah. "His disciples."

"So-called. I ran from them and hid my fear from
those stone-throwers—"

"But they didn't."

"They would have, I tell you. Or they would have
made their observations known to those among my
people, who would have. Same difference. Same. So,
I beat them at their game." Abatal looked up at Jesus.
"Sorry, my Lord. No reflection on you. Only me. And
them. And . . ." She bowed her head in shame. "So, I
preempted them. I ran into town before them and
declared to anyone who would listen, *'Come, see this*

man who has told me everything I have done. Could he be the Messiah?'"

"But what was there to fear? Really. You were already living as an outcast: unmarried, with a man."

"True. An unveiled Samaritan woman does not fear for her life in the same way as those among your people."

"Stonings are rare in Judea."

"There are many kinds of stonings among you Judeans."

"Hmm. True."

"As well as for Samaritans. All of them lead to a kind of emptiness—and death. Men. They possess us into invisibility. Even within ourselves." She exhaled thoughtfully. "Anyway. I succeeded in my invisibility. Many of those who heard me speaking about the Anointed One went to meet him because I told them. I told them that, *'He told me everything I ever did.'* That's what I kept saying to anyone who would listen."

"Did it work?"

"I'm here, aren't I?" Abatal grinned. "And they believed in him because of my humble, woman's testimony, which usually has no meaning unless men have something to gain."

"What would that have been?"

Abatal winced. "I don't know. But my people believe in a coming Messiah."

"So do mine."

"And my people respect their prophets."

"So do mine."

"But yours are often avoided in their own time."

"That's not true," Ephah said defensively.

"Hmm. Well. Typically, only the outcasts among you are the ones who listen."

"You mean, the poor."

"No difference. Your people believe that you're far from your God if you're poor." Abatal snickered. "Funny."

"What?"

"My people begged him to stay with them. And he did. For two days. Because they half-believed in what I said."

"Why half?"

"Because after they listened to him, one of them, a man, made it a point to tell me that he believed in Jesus for what Jesus said, not for what I said. This man had to make it clear to me that Jesus' words were not tainted by the declaration of a woman." Her eyes darkened. "The petty scoundrel. No woman was going to get the best of him. No woman was going to be the first to discover the Messiah among us." She spoke softly into Ephah's ear to dramatize her point. "The man even whispered his remark to me in order to divest any power to my public claim. He said, *'I— we—believe now, not because of your testimony. But now that I've heard him for myself, I—we—realize that he really is the savior of the world.'*" Ephah turned to her in astonishment. Abatal banished any growing doubt. "It's true. And I quickly heeded. I knew I was walking on fragile ground. So, I disappeared. And now, here I am. Among silent women and, therefore, upon fragile ground."

"Is there any other kind of ground in this world?"

"No. But men deny that by stamping their feet. They think what they see and hear and feel is the truth. The truth. What is truth?"

Lightning scorched the ground at the north end of Golgotha. The explosion terrified many.

Young women screamed. Children screeched. Matrons trembled.

"We are present. See?" Ephah sighed. "Everywhere you look, there are women and children. That is the truth. And yet, men will say that he died alone." Ephah walked away from Abatal and approached the foot of the cross. Jesus was unconscious. "You are not abandoned, my Lord. Invisible women are here with you. We are present." She glanced at John's crumbled figure at the foot of the stake. "And we stand before you cloaked by our love for you."

Abatal approached her. "Who are you?"

"A woman once possessed."

"Ha. Good one, Abatal. You've been speaking to a mad woman."

"Men drive us into madness." Ephah lowered her mantle and exposed her wet hair. "And yet, a man drove the madness out of me." She looked at Jesus. "Possess me. Possess me!" She dropped to her knees.

Abatal stooped down to her. "Ephah. Ephah. Control yourself. Please." She assisted Ephah to her feet and held her steady.

Mud soiled the lower portion of Ephah's tunic. "He was speaking in a synagogue on a Sabbath day."

"What were you doing in a synagogue?"

"Women have their place there if they want."

"Hmm. Go on."

"For eighteen years I was afflicted by this . . . this dark spirit."

"You mean, demon—"

"Madness. All the same." Ephah exhaled. "I . . . I was crippled by this . . . this possession inside of me. I was bent over and unable to straighten up even a little. I was almost unable to walk. I never knew what I was doing. I wasn't myself. And on that day, like any other, I didn't know what I was doing. In fact, I still don't know how I got to that synagogue." Ephah sighed. "Anyway. Anyway. I . . . I was desperate. I . . . I wanted to cry out, but He—He noticed me first. His. His eyes. His eyes." She studied Jesus' face. "Where are his eyes now?" She bowed her head. "He called me over to him and waited until I was within his reach. Then he said, *'Woman, you are free from your sickness,'* and laid his hands on me: his right hand upon my head and his left upon my shoulder. I opened my mouth and exhaled deeply, then . . . then I felt myself present and before him. And in praise of God, I straightened up. I straightened up after eighteen years of demon possession. Eighteen!" She cried.

Abatal spread her arms toward the sky feeling vindicated. "Woman. Woman. You see? He was equal to woman."

Ephah's eyes filled with tears. "Yes. You know that directly. You've proven that to me with your story. And, therefore, you've earned my trust. You've earned the knowledge of my own story, which I usually keep hidden."

"My story. Your story." Abatal lowered her arms with a newly found serenity. "Imagine that. A Jew and a Samaritan are now sisters."

Anger surfaced from Ephah, in contrast to Abatal's calm. "Men. Those at the synagogue became angry at Jesus because he had healed me on the Sabbath. Hypocrites. The leader of the synagogue didn't care about me. All he cared about was his Sabbath Law. I was nothing to him. My suffering meant nothing to him. He as much as said so to those present, as if I were nothing, when he so arrogantly dismissed me by saying, *'There are six days in which we are to work. Come back here on one of those days to be healed. Not now. Not on the Sabbath.'* I wanted to spit on his face." Ephah's expression softened momentarily. "But, Jesus. Dear, dear, Jesus." Her eyes smoldered with the satisfaction of her recollection. "He spat words at the synagogue leader in my defense, and scolded that dismissive man into shame before all those listening in the synagogue by saying, *'You fake!'* Then Jesus stood silently for a long time and disarmed every man present with his penetrating eyes. The tension was enormous. I was frightened. He was not. The steady quality of his anger was unlike any I had ever heard: *'You fakes!'* This time, he included all of them. Then he declared, *'All of you untie your beasts from the feeding troughs on the Sabbath day and lead them to water, don't you?'* Then Jesus took my hand. My hand." Her eyes grew wide with pride.

"I . . . I felt like a queen. I . . . I was not ashamed to stand before these men who would have discarded me—no—much worse. The Sabbath. Much, much worse, I think." She shook her head. "Anyway. Anyway. He presented me. *'This woman. A descendant of Abraham whom Satan bound for eighteen long years. Shouldn't she be released from her bonds, as well, on the Sabbath day?'* I held my breath. And to my astonishment, several men rejoiced." She exhaled to emphasize her astonishment even now. "After a few moments, others cheered. And as they cheered, Jesus released my hand and allowed me to disappear among them. From that moment, it became about Jesus and this synagogue ruler. Then it became about them. And as Jesus spoke to these men, I eased toward the back of the synagogue unnoticed. God. I was so relieved, but still—so, so frightened." She pressed the palms of her hands against her breast in order to calm herself. "Jesus spoke to them about mustard seeds and leaven and God's imperial rule. I don't know. I was too exhilarated and scared and nervous to hear anything else he had to say. Anyway. Anyway. When I reached a door, I ran out of the synagogue as if my good fortune would be taken away if I didn't truly disappear. So, I ran and hid and . . . and remembered his eyes, his touch, his gentle voice, his power over me." Ephah raised her sodden mantle over her head and regarded Abatal with a sudden and equal calm. "This concludes my humble story. Not much of one. Little thought of. Little known."

The rainfall intensified.

Abatal and Ephah drew closer to seek each other's comfort. Their stillness together became part of Golgotha's landscape.

CHAPTER 8

Women of Golgotha

Golgotha, the place of the skull, was a rocky bulge in the terrain near the city's wall that separated Jerusalem from this barren place of torture and death and sorrowful women.

Blessed Mother of Jesus stirred. The numerous circles of women standing at the periphery of her immediate inner circle of influence—Mary of Magdala on her right side, and Blessed Mother's sister, the mother of James and Joses and wife of Clopus on her left side—felt the origin of her emotions.

The cause of Blessed Mary's physical agitation was not the increase in rain. Not the intensity of thunder. Not the shock of lightning. Not the severity of the trembling earth.

Only sorrow. Only sorrow.

The closest circle of women stood on the left side of Blessed Mother. This small group of women, second only to the inner circle, felt Blessed Mother's sorrow most acutely, being mothers, all mothers themselves: Mara, Peter's wife and mother of Eli; Merab, Peter's mother; Shelomith, Peter's mother-in-law; Salome, mother of the sons of Zebedee, James, and John; and Hanna, wife of Aaron and two months away from first born motherhood.

Another group of women, third in so-called stature, stood behind the inner circle, like maternal sentinels, prepared to protect Blessed Mother's privacy. They were strong women, good women, devoted women: Joanna, the wife of Chuza and the manager of Herod's household; Lazarus's sisters, Mary and Martha; and Susanna, the wealthy widow, who provided for Jesus and his disciples out of her resources during his time on the road, where he preached among the people. Despite her continued monetary support, his crucifixion reduced the power of her wealth among her sister disciples and, therefore, reduced her importance.

The other circles of women were grouped into a variety of associations: the loyal Women of Galilee, the Daughters of Jerusalem, the Elders from the countryside, and the hopeful peasants and indigents with nowhere else to go. This was the approximate hierarchy among the Women of Golgotha.

Some of the sister disciples vied for Blessed Mother's attention; others sought greater approval; several maneuvered for an increased standing with her. Blessed Mother's placement into John's household, by her son, raised Salome's status by several degrees. Now, Salome anticipated her inclusion within the inner circle, and hoped to gain the confidence of Blessed Sister and Mary of Magdala. This was the occult politics over Jesus' love.

Outside the civilized labyrinth of sister disciples and outside the feeble light created by the legionnaires' torches, ragged spectators kept their distance like hungry dogs; this riffraff was the last remnant of what orbited around the earlier, wealthy crowd that sought entertainment. Those who lurked in this outer darkness were also relatives of the carrion birds that waited for the opportunity to pick over the bones of the dead.

A woman from among the Daughters of Jerusalem approached Blessed Mary, Mother of Jesus. "You have other sons."

"A mother loves all her children," said Blessed Mother. "Still—my first born is more than a son."

"Yes. More than a son," said this Daughter of Jerusalem. She stepped closer to Blessed Mother. "I know he had power. I experienced it firsthand. From my sick bed. Deep within my soul. Instantly. I knew he . . . he was the Messiah. My Master. My Lord. I knew I . . . I would do anything for him. Anything."

Several rocks were hurled at them. Several rocks were hurled at HIM. At HIM.

The Daughter of Jerusalem misunderstood Mary of Magdala's sudden anger, and thought she may have intruded upon the sanctity of the inner circle too long.

Mary of Magdala straightened her back as she addressed Blessed Mother. "I will stand on this mound with you to the end of time, if necessary, to protect him from the wild beasts of the night and to protect him from those who would further desecrate what's left of his body." She took several aggressive steps away from the emotional security of Blessed Mother's side toward the unknown desecrator of her Lord: riffraff-thieves and violent beings of no means. "Get away! I may not be able to defend him from Roman legionnaires or from Herodian guards, but I'll defend him from anyone else!"

The Daughter of Jerusalem crept back to her circle of women to disassociate herself from Mary's rage.

Mary blinked her eyes several times to regain focus. "Sorry." She turned to Blessed Sister and whispered, "Sorry." She sought Blessed Mother's gentle eyes. "Sorry."

Blessed Mother extended her right arm and invited Mary back to her side. Mary obeyed.

An intense slash of lightning across the angry sky forced many to cower.

Blessed Mother and Blessed Sister and Mary of Magdala were impervious to the threatening elements. Merab and Salome and the others in their devoted circle, as well as Joanna and Susanna and those in their immediate group were not as secure about themselves and their personal safety as the hallowed nucleus of three. Therefore, they sought comfort from one another with sympathetic eyes and clinging hands.

Golgotha's premature darkness did not resemble twilight. Lightning cut deep streaks across the threatening sky, and thunder injected terror into the hearts of the ragged outer circles of women, who stood near the shadow of their dying Rabbi, Master, Lord. The loyal Women of Galilee, the Elders from the countryside, and the Daughters of Jerusalem, including Greeks, Samaritans, adulterers, and common peasants—all—responded with cries. Fortunately, the strength, the silence, the stillness of the hallowed nucleus of three, prevented these sister disciples from submitting to panic.

The steep angle of the rain pelted Susanna's face as she looked into the dark sky with a wild desperation equal to the ferocity of the unrelenting circular wind. She felt the increased loss of her wealthy importance with every assault from the sky, the heavens, the powers above—all directed at her, she thought, all taunting her loss of status, status, status, which could be seen in the way her subtracted figure slumped. Once again, Susanna had been stripped from herself. But this time, Jesus was not able to offer her his love and support. She was alone. And even though she was beautiful and dark-haired, blue-eyed and delicately built, she appeared physically reduced.

Susanna had to seek comfort or go mad. "Blessed Mother. Blessed Mother. Comfort me. Protect me from this inner turmoil. Please."

Blessed Mother turned to her, despite her own suffering, and bowed her head—the transmission of sympathy calmed Susanna.

As soon as Blessed Mother directed her gaze upon her crucified son, Susanna released her grip from the front of her soggy tunic and dripping cloak and drooping mantle. The three fabrics unraveled, despite their rain-soaked condition, and hung straight down.

The sky flickered like a harassed candle and illuminated Jesus' thorn-crowned and bloody head. Susanna's hard-won calmness was not a permanent condition.

The veil that covered the lower portion of her face intensified the sternness in her black eyes. She looked like an ageless penitent separated from the world by her leprosy. Her rough wool was worn to the thinness of linen, and where continued repair of the garment seemed impossible, further repair was likely. The burden of her disease did not diminish her determined posture, which demanded respect and respectability. "Men!"

"Shh."

"This is where we've been brought to?"

"We've traveled no distance," said an elderly woman, who also had leprosy.

"Literal. You're too damned literal," said the veiled penitent.

"I'm practical. Having babies is literal."

"You old fool. Having babies has no value to men."

"Until there aren't. I've been a grandmother. I should know." The elderly woman cackled. The three teeth in her mouth had color variations of yellow, brown, and black.

"Childbirth costs us everything. Childbirth gives us everything. Women. We are lost."

"We are mothers."

"We are lepers, you fool."

Hanna stepped away from the safety of the second circle of influence. "We are not lost."

"You know nothing, my child," said the elderly woman.

"Hanna, come back here," said Merab, excitedly. "They have leprosy."

"Do you fear us?" The elderly woman displayed her three teeth with a kindly smile. "We do have leprosy."

"She's afraid," said the veiled penitent.

Hanna stepped closer to them.

"Do you fear us?" the elderly woman repeated.

Hanna ignored Merab's plea for her return. "No. Not you. Or you. But I do fear, dear Grandmother."

"Ahh." The endearment touched the elderly woman. "What do you fear, young lady?"

"What I've suddenly come to realize."

"Ahh, a parable. She's begun a parable," said the veiled penitent.

The elderly woman ignored her sister. "And your realization is?"

"That there is no other way out of my condition than to bear—"

"Ahh, yes, yes." The elderly woman nodded sentimentally. "You'll bear. I can see you've come to realize that after seven months—it is seven months."

"Yes."

"Yes, yes. That's about when I had that realization with my first child. You are in reach of a woman's knowledge."

"Until then," said the veiled penitent, "you're still a girl."

Hanna looked at Jesus' torn body hanging on the wood. "How does he know? How does he understand our pain?"

"He's still a man," said the veiled penitent. "He knows nothing of a woman's pain."

"He was kind to all the mother's of the world." Hanna stepped between the two lepers.

Merab ventured a single step away from the group. "Hanna, think of your baby."

"If you're so concerned about her, come and take her." The veiled penitent stepped toward Merab. "Come. Take her."

"We won't hurt the child," said the elderly woman. "You must know that." She indicated Jesus' presence. "You must know that."

Merab retreated, then dissolved into the group's safety feeling embarrassed.

"I did not mean to humiliate her," said the elderly woman.

Hanna was touched by her concern for Merab. "She often humiliates herself, Grandmother."

"Ahh. You're such a dear. Grandmother. I haven't enjoyed hearing that in years." She noted Hanna's sorrow. "Nor have I seen such gentle tears."

"I don't mean to embarrass you. I don't mean to."

"Child, you can't embarrass us. We . . . we are at the end of ourselves. See?"

"We're lepers," said the veiled penitent. "We're nobody."

Hanna beheld the elderly woman. "The past." Then she indicated an adolescent girl among the Daughters of Jerusalem. "The future." She touched her round abdomen. "The present. And, I fear." She glanced at Jesus. "Despite our Master's promise. Despite his miracles."

"If only I'd been able to touch him before he was crucified," said the veiled penitent.

"Shush," said the elderly woman. She smiled at Hanna. "Go on, my child."

"Despite the knowledge of his . . . his . . ." Hanna's tears prevented her from speaking further.

"Child. Child. I'd caress you but—" The elderly woman gazed at Jesus. "We *are* leper scum."

"No. You are women of God," Hanna declared. "Holy sisters. Disciples of our dying Lord."

"We are leper scum," the veiled penitent insisted.

"No. You are women. The world is blind—"

"And has made us invisible, my child." The elderly woman's lips trembled.

Hanna bowed her head. "Where else can holiness be seen?"

The toothless, elderly woman sank to her knees as if she were having heart difficulties. She pressed both hands against her breast. "Dear, God. You've reduced me to holiness, dear sister. My nothingness cannot be seen, but it has been felt by you, my dear little mother, who is filled with life."

Hanna peered at Jesus. "It is he . . . he is filled with life." She touched her large abdomen. "Didn't he claim to take death away?"

"I heard, yes, he . . . he whispered such . . . such nonsense."

"Nonsense," the veiled penitent vehemently agreed.

The elderly woman rose unsteadily to her feet. "He whispered—"

"Life-giving forces," said Hanna.

"I know, I know—"

"He's going to be dead," said the veiled penitent.

"Yes. Yes, he is," said Hanna.

"Then . . . then you know nothing more than we do," said the veiled penitent in triumph.

"I confess."

"Nothing. We are still nothing," the veiled penitent insisted.

"Through the intimacy of God's will, we bring babies into the world who possess eternal souls." Hanna touched the elderly woman's arm. "I confess."

The old leper pulled her arm away, startled by the

touch of someone who was clean. "Bless you, my child. Bless you for his word."

She and Hanna gazed at Jesus, while the veiled penitent continued her protests against Hanna and the world and that man.

The infant's cry forced a mother to maneuver her baby underneath her cloak, reach for herself with her free hand, and guide the baby's mouth to her nipple.

Another woman, pregnant, needed to find a place to sit. A kind sister from Galilee noted her distress, removed her own cloak despite the chill, and laid it on the muddy ground, double folded. The Galilean woman gestured at the cloak to convey her offer of help.

"I can't let you do that," said the pregnant woman.

"And I can't allow you to sit in the mud. Besides, my cloak is already soaked and it can only provide you with marginal comfort."

The pregnant woman faltered with exhaustion. "Are you sure—"

"Here. Let me assist you. Please."

The pregnant woman was too weary to resist the Galilean's help. "I shouldn't have come here."

"There's nowhere else to go." She assisted the lady onto her cloak.

"Hmm." Relief from her discomfort was immediate. "Yes. Yes. You're right. Nowhere to go. Nowhere to go."

The Galilean sat beside the pregnant woman. "And no place to sit. Ahh. This cloak is like a wet sponge."

The pregnant woman touched her abdomen with the palm of her left hand, then urinated on herself. "I'm sorry. I've relieved myself on your cloak."

"Water. You've only passed water. Besides, who can smell anything in all this stench of death and rain?"

The pregnant woman peeked over her shoulder, then sighed.

"Don't feel embarrassed," said the Galilean. "Nobody cares about someone else's private difficulties."

"You're very kind. I . . . I thank you."

"I've three children of my own. Over there, with my sister." She tapped the pregnant woman's arm. "I've lost control of my water a time or two, believe me."

The pregnant woman smiled gratefully. When she leaned on her right arm, her elbow sank deeply into the mush of the cloak beneath her. "The end of the world. That's what it feels like."

The Galilean sighed. "I don't care." After glancing at the two unimportant crosses staked on the hillside, she studied Jesus' tortured figure nailed to the wood. All that was left of him was an empty shell. "I don't care."

"Why do you insist on carrying that small jar, my sister?"

"This is spikenard oil to cleanse him with."

"Dear, God. Those Roman's will never allow you to do that."

"I'll get this on him somehow."

"But . . . but why that lotion?"

"It's left over from when I cleansed his feet with—"

"Ahh—your hair."

"What?"

"You dried his feet of the lotion's excess with your hair. Shameful."

"It was not. I'm surprised you're still jealous, Martha. He was a dinner guest at our brother's home. And I offered him—"

"Yourself, Mary. Shameful."

"Think what you like, my sister. But I'm glad I acted on my feelings. Unlike you."

Martha held her temper. "You always have your way."

"And you're always pointing your resentful finger at me. But our Lord was glad I did that. He said he wanted me to keep what was left, for the time when his body needed cleansing."

Martha yielded. "Yes. Yes."

"He said that the poor would always be around, but he wouldn't be." She stared at Jesus on the cross. "I'm here now."

Martha softened. "We both are."

Mary pressed her small jar of spikenard oil against her breast. "And my lotion will cleanse his feet again."

"If you say so, my dear. If you say so." Heaven rumbled and deepened Martha's terror. "Lord, this thunder."

"Angels, my sister. I heard angels."

John howled like an injured dog, then banged his head against the wood of his Rabbi's stake.

Mara nudged Salome's upper left arm. "What's happened to your John? Look at him."

"I don't know."

"But he's your son," Mara whispered.

"Who can't be helped," Salome countered, with irritation. "Any more than our Blessed Mother can help her son."

Mara cleared her throat. "I'm . . . I'm sorry."

"You . . . you need to tend to your own house. At least one of my sons has remained at the foot of our Rabbi's cross."

"I'm sorry. I deserved that."

Salome's anger softened. "I resent my own helplessness, and my son's madness."

"Don't. Don't say that."

"Why? Because you have a mad husband who is also afraid of what the Romans will do to him?"

Mara sighed. "Yes." She glanced at John's pitiful figure slumped against the base of Jesus' cross. "At least John is present. We are not."

Salome averted her eyes from Mara. "And if we are not seen because we are women, can it be said that we are truly here? Can it be said that we are brave?"

The intense honesty between them undressed their shame.

Salome studied her son's pathetic figure. "I'd be wrong no matter what I tried to do for him or for his brother, James."

"True."

"Still, I would help my sons if I could make a difference."

"You're a woman, who'd humiliate them further. Believe me, I know. My husband Peter and I, well—" Mara touched Salome's shoulder. "Nobody can help John, except John."

"Nobody can help anybody."

Quiet tears streamed down Mara's cheeks. "What's to become of us?"

Her tunic was made of dark brown sackcloth, worn not because of mourning but because of abject poverty. A head hole and a pair of arm holes were cut into the shapeless garment to accommodate the untidy woman. The garment was drawn to the body with a belt made from a length of discarded rope tied around her waist and held in place with a crude knot. The thick nails of her bare feet were black and chipped and caked with mud. "He took away my sense of public disgrace even though I am lame. He washed away my . . . my insecurity about myself, my worth, my status, my . . . my disgrace." Her body became rigid. "Damn all those for the smallness of their minds." She relaxed. "I'm still a woman. As full and as virtuous as any woman who has sons and daughters and a contented husband." She leaned against her wooden crutch. "Jesus saw that I was a woman. Equal to any by my humbleness of spirit." She suddenly felt embarrassed. "Well, perhaps not so humble. But a woman nonetheless. And, well, perhaps not perfect. But I've reduced my anger and resentment against men. And the Law. Even my envy is not as intense whenever I see a mother with her children, whenever I'm reminded that I haven't felt a baby jump in my womb, or whenever I'm shunned at the well because of my lameness." Her eyes deepened as she squinted. "Yes. Imperfect. I'm a cripple. And I savor my lowly status as His slave." She sighed. "I . . . I no longer sit in darkness. I know the Lord is with me. Me." She took a difficult step toward Jesus. "You do not see me as a cripple. You see me."

"Eloi, Eloi, lema sabachthani?"

The earth quaked like an aching newborn exploding into being: confused and trembling and bordering between life and death.

Those who were afraid of the shaking earth, felt split apart. Those who were not afraid, seemed to be awakened.

Everywhere one looked, there were signs. Signs:

The blanket of darkness.

The rolling clouds above.

The lightning tearing the heavens in two.

The disappearance of the sun's body.

The torn curtains within.

The splitting of the hardest of hearts.

The feminine determination to remain on Golgotha.

Signs. Signs. Signs.

"Eloi, Eloi, lema sabachthani?"

An expectant mother in her eighth month approached the cross. Her mantle framed the wildness in her eyes. Her lips tightened with anger. Her hard eyes cast disdain upon the man nailed to the cross. "Serves him right. My husband abandoned me to follow in the light of that Galilean. He was promised the Kingdom of Heaven at the expense of ordinary life."

The embittered woman lowered her mantle and exposed her long, wet, tangled hair. She touched her bulbous abdomen. She appeared more malnourished than expectant. "What manner of trading is this? What kind of magic spell can erase the love between a man and a woman?"

She squatted with difficulty, then reached for a rock. "Ahh."

She stood up with equal difficulty, then threw the stone at Jesus. It glanced off the foot of Jesus' cross. "I know I'll never see him again because I saw it in his eyes. *'You're no substitute for everlasting life.'*"

She squatted with greater difficulty, and grabbed another rock. "I hate that Galilean: he robbed the father of my unborn and left us with hunger."

She raised her arm to throw the stone.

"Drop it!" ordered one of the Roman guards.

She dropped the stone.

"Your first one almost hit me, damn you! You'll pay with your life with the second!"

She reached for her swollen belly with both her hands.

"I said get back, damn you!"

She backed away from the guard and the cross. She stumbled.

A Judean woman prevented her from falling. "Are you all right?"

The expectant mother glimpsed at her. "Who are you?" She considered her surroundings. "Where am I?" She broke free of the Judean woman, then faltered.

The Judean caught hold of her once again. "There, there. Don't be afraid of me. I've got you." She placed the palm of her left hand on the expectant mother's forehead. "You have a fever. How do you feel?"

"Feel? Feel?" She searched her memory. "I didn't feel quite so bitter after I threw that stone and hit the foot of his cross during the time of darkness. People were frightened, but I knew better: this was no man of God."

The Judean caressed the sick and broken mother. "You poor dear."

"Who are you? Where am I?"

"In the time of darkness."

"Oh. Yes. The darkness. The darkness is all that's left."

"Eloi, Eloi, lema sabachthani?"

"Children. Children! Gather around more closely. Come on. More closely, I said. Come. Come." Despite the head matron's repeated attempts to gather the children, bedlam prevailed. She saw an unattended child from the corner of her right eye. "Ruth. Look. Catch her before she strays too far." The matron in charge was worried about the Roman guards, who had little patience with women and children. "Hodesh, stay alert. The children are nervous."

"Ada, I believe you're the one who's nervous," said Hodesh, whose attention was divided between the crying baby in her arms and the weight of the swaddled infant tied to her back.

"Dear, God. You're right," said Ada, wife of Elraam and mother of Amasa, Rachel, and Reba. The matron studied the active, crying, hungry children. She softened her authority. "That gift from God you have swaddled on your back is beautiful."

Hodesh shifted the baby in her arms. "Thank you." She noticed movement from the corner of her left eye. "Leah. Leah. Watch your baby brother." She stooped momentarily to relieve the weight on her back. She felt confidant that her swaddled infant was warm and safe and growing straight. "Agh." She straightened up. "My baby boy is as solid and as heavy as a block of stone." She stretched her back, then saw Ruth. "I wish Ruth was more help with the children." Hodesh grabbed a young girl by the hand. "Stay with me, child."

"Leave Ruth alone," said another woman. "Look at me. I'm a midwife, not a baby-sitter. I'm not doing such a great job here, either. We're all trying to do our best."

"Maacah is right," said Ada. "Besides, she's nursing a sick baby. Very sick. I'm not sure . . ." Ada avoided finishing the thought.

Hodesh nodded with understanding.

"Benjamin. Come here." Maacah caressed her seven-year-old son. "Stay close to me. Your mother needs you."

Ada and Hodesh, Maacah and Ruth, and the other women tending to the children on Golgotha suddenly heard Jesus' plaintive voice carry through the wind and the rain and the darkness.

"What did he say?" Ada demanded. "What did he say?"

"*'Eloi, Eloi,'*" said Ruth. She threw a hopeful glance at Hodesh. "Did you hear the rest?"

Hodesh nodded. "*'Lema sabachthani?'*"

"Ohhh." Ruth cuddled her sick, suckling baby. "*'My God, my God.'*" She looked at her baby with increased anxiety. "*'Why have you abandoned me?'*" She searched the faces of the other women. "My God. Where does that leave us, if he is abandoned?"

"This cannot be," said Ada. "This cannot be the thing we are to understand."

"He was one of us," said Hodesh.

"Yes. Yes." Ada's mind reeled with conflicting thoughts. "And if he is our Lord, then . . . then there is no escape from this . . . this life of suffering."

"He did not come to bring us comfort," Maacah interjected. "He said that to us many times. Don't you remember? Don't you remember?"

"Yes!" Ada snapped irritably. She ground her teeth. "Yes."

"What's that?" Hodesh inquired. "What's that?"

The children inhaled with anxiety, then exhaled with exhaustion.

"That was Jesus, again," said Maacah. She caressed her seven-year-old son.

"What did he say, Maacah?"

"I . . . I couldn't hear the words, I couldn't—"

"He's dying," said Ruth, in monotone. "He's finally near his end." Ruth pulled her baby away from her breast. The infant began to cry.

"Ahh." Hodesh caressed the young girl she had by the hand. "We are not alone."

"And neither is our Master," Ruth whispered.

The darkness increased, but they did not feel abandoned. Only cold and frightened.

"Eloi, Eloi, lema sabachthani?"

A robust woman tightened her cloak around her when she heard Jesus' final words. "*'My God, my God . . .'*" The woman shivered. "I'm glad I broke open that

alabaster jar and poured all the oil on his head. I'm
glad I offered him comfort before this . . . this death."

"I envy you, Agia," said the woman standing
nearby, her eyes wide with fear of the growing darkness and abandonment within her.

"He did not flinch from me, Tirzah, even though
he said I made him ready for burial."

"Burial? But—"

"That's what he said."

"But—"

"I offered myself to him and still, somehow, he . . .
he raised me above myself before his . . . his disciples—before the world."

Tirzah grew concerned. "Are you all right, Agia?"

"He did not flinch when the oil ran down his
neck."

"Agia."

"He smiled deeply. Suggestively."

"You're scaring me."

"In fact, he took such great pleasure in my offer
that . . . that he excited me."

"My God, not him."

Agia faced the emptiness of Jesus' body. "Why
not? He is a man. And I'm a woman."

"Is he dead, Agia? Is he dead?" A cold wind blew
through them. "I'm scared. Is this the end?"

Agia caressed Tirzah without concealing her rap-
ture. "He nearly brought me to . . . to ecstasy."

"Agia!" She pulled away from her disturbed sister.

"It was not his fault."

"Stop it. How can you be thinking of such a thing at a time like this?"

"Calm yourself. We're all doomed. At least, I am. And I don't care."

Tirzah wrung her hands. "Agia, please, you're frightening me."

"He's dying." Agia shrugged her shoulders. "And the truth is the truth. My feelings for him won't change this bad weather or these dark conditions or his bitter death. The truth exists."

Tirzah burst into tears. "What is the truth?"

Agia pressed her forehead against Tirzah's left temple. "You do want the truth, don't you? Don't you?"

"There . . . there are limits," said Tirzah.

Agia pushed her away. "Then you're a hypocrite, and I'll have nothing more to do with you."

Tirzah was terrified. "Please. I'm sorry. Please don't abandon me."

"You think me mad."

"No," she lied. "No. I don't."

"I'll not back away from him."

"All right. All right. Anything you say." Tirzah wrapped her left arm around Agia's waist. Her mad sister responded with reluctant affection. "I'm exposed. I'm . . . I'm only a woman."

"Be proud."

"How? Sometimes I . . . I wish I were a man."

"Men." The contempt in Agia's voice was equal to the ferocity in the changing earth elements that surrounded them. Tirzah held onto Agia, as the earth shook beneath them. "They drank his blood at his Seder table, which I helped to set. Last night, they drank his blood to commemorate another kind of Passover."

"Agia. Please. That's revolting."

"That's because I talk of men."

"You talk of blood and—"

"Men. They can drink his blood, in whatever form, but they'll blanch at the mere mention of a woman's blood. The blood of life. The blood of love. Menstrual blood."

Tirzah was paralyzed: shocked by Agia's madness, and frightened by the unworldly elements from above and below.

"We are less than nothing while we are menstruating. And we remain nothing until we are beyond our white days. Why should our blood be ritually impure? God made us, as well. God made us!" Agia gazed lovingly at Jesus. "He knew that his blood, the blood of man, came from a woman's blood. He knew that we brought man's blood to life."

Tirzah continued listening to her sister with greater unresponsiveness. She held onto Agia's madness because there was nowhere else to go. No place to seek the increase in comfort. Tirzah's thoughts reduced her to emptiness:

Oh, God. Oh, God. Is this all the comfort I can expect? Is this all there is?

Tirzah held onto her sister with all her strength.

"Eloi, Eloi, lema sabachthani?"

The tight cliques of loyal women sustained their vigilance around the crosses of the three men. The Daughters of Jerusalem and the Women of Galilee in particular maintained their devotion to Blessed Mother and her inner and outer circles of eminent sister disciples.

The dark and dull tones of brown and tan were the dominant woolen colors worn by these plainly dressed figures in mourning. An occasional bit of embroidery could be seen on the tassel-end of a mantle or two, and a rare spot of red appeared in some of the striped patterns and simple geometric designs that were woven into the fabric of a few woolen tunics and mantles and cloaks and, therefore, provided some visual relief from the almost standard uniform of poverty reflected by the threadbare condition of their garments.

Two creatures, poor and unknown, stood outside the main groups of sister disciples. They were so ragged and destitute, so malnourished and diseased that they were invisible even among women. Among lepers, only among lepers could they hope to be equal.

Neither one of them wore mantles or sandals, neither one had a belt to tie their sackcloth around their waist. The taller woman had open sores and lesions on her skin. The shorter one had large patches of hair missing from her head.

The shorter woman scratched one of the bald spots on her scalp. "Some prophet that Nazarene turned out to be."

The taller one cackled loudly. "What do you expect, Haggith? They have spat on him and have flogged him. They have violated and tortured him."

"Rome's way: they spit and flog, rape and kill for pleasure. Animals. Pagan animals."

"Careful, Haggith. We're not that invisible."

"Ahh."

"Not where Rome's cruelty is concerned. How can you forget?"

"Four Roman legionnaires. How can I forget what those animals did to me?" Haggith clenched her teeth bitterly to hold back her tears. "Don't remind me, Bathshua, of something I can never forget. I was beautiful once."

"And I had a husband and . . . and I did not escape their brutality. None of us did in our village."

"Murderers. Rapists. Look at us, now."

"We're alive."

"Disgraced and broken. Diseased and thrown away. This is not living." Haggith studied the crucified men. Then studied the man that groveled at the foot of Jesus' cross. "That sniveling one at his feet thinks he understands suffering."

"He's a man. What else?"

Haggith laughed cynically. "He better watch out. Rome will provide him a true reason for suffering. He'll end up crucified himself."

"I believe that pathetic one is mimicking the Messiah's silence."

"Messiah, Messiah. Don't hold your breath, Bathshua. You really believe that nonsense? Ha. And you really believe that the other madman at his foot has the presence of mind to mimic?"

"Well, it appears to me that—"

"Bah." Haggith sneered at John. "He knows nothing. Nothing." She studied Jesus. "And the other, bah. His suffering is nearly over."

"What about the other two men?"

"They're also being murdered by Pilate. What of it? Their suffering is almost over as well."

"Not for the big one."

"Soon, Bathshua. Can't you see his suffering is near its end? But not ours, you simple-hearted creature. How far do you need to be broken? How can you disregard your misery and hunger so easily?"

"I'm hungry. Yes."

"You're dying, yes," Haggith mimicked. Then mumbled, "Suffering, suffering." Her resentment transformed into anger. "I've suffered more than that mongrel Galilean!"

"Haggith. Why are—?"

"And you've suffered more, as well! So don't ask me any more stupid questions." Haggith pursed her broken lips, then smiled mischievously. "I do know one thing." She drew closer to Bathshua. "Each one of us is about ourselves."

It took several moments for Bathshua's confusion to surface. She picked at one of her scabs. The tone in her voice sounded childish. "Love one another is what he was supposed to have said. Love one another—"

"Is still about ourselves."

"I don't know, Haggith. You're frightening me."

"Me. Look at those three nailed on the wood. That's what you should be afraid of: Rome. And look at that dog groveling at your so-called Messiah's feet." Her disdain for the tenets of *love one another* poured out of her. "That one's forgotten himself. That should frighten you more."

"Everything frightens me, right now. Everything. I keep trying to hold onto the things Jesus said that day we saw him. Do you remember when he said to that paralyzed man?—'*Mister, your sins have been forgiven you.*'"

"I was there." Haggith spat on the ground. "I saw that man get up and walk—"

"After. After Jesus forgave his sins."

"I know, I know, and I'm still confused."

"Jesus said it was easier."

"Than what? Explain it to me."

"Well." Bathshua's constant hunger had weakened her ability to reason, had reduced her capacity to remember clearly. "He said . . . he said it was easier to forgive than to walk."

"But he did both."

"Then maybe, maybe he was showing us to ourselves." Bathshua suddenly spoke with authority. "Maybe he was demonstrating that we can forgive anything. Any of us. Like him. And that's easier than healing ourselves physically."

"Hmm. Tell that to the rich."

"We are equal to them."

"Hmm. I don't know."

"He said so."

"And I don't understand how you got all that from his few words."

"You weren't listening."

"I saw what I saw."

"I know—"

"And it confuses me."

"I know."

Haggith scratched a raw bald spot on the left side of her head. "Where did you get this sudden authority?"

"I . . . I'm simply remembering. I . . . I don't know."

"Yes. Well. I'm hungry. And your Messiah is as good as dead." Haggith's harsh tone made Bathshua shudder. "God permits Rome's presence. Rome killed him. Therefore, God killed him."

With her right hand, she held the lower left side of her mantle above her nose to shield the lower portion of her face. Her eyes peered over the veil with a deep and dark intensity.

"Eloi, Eloi, lema sabachthani?"

The shock of the moment made her drop the mantle from her face and step toward Jesus' final moments.

Another woman reached out to stop her, but accidentally pulled her mantle completely off instead. She ran to her sister and returned the mantle.

The bareheaded sister stared at the garment as if

she did not comprehend what she had in her hand. Her long black hair was braided into a single strand, which pulled her hair away from her face and forehead, and exposed the full force of her unusual beauty. The subtle and silky Asian elements of her countenance were at odds with her heavier Semitic features. Her face and forehead were flat and her thin chin protruded delicately to a distinct point. Her silvery blue eyes were large, her down-turned nose was strong, and the lips of her small mouth were fleshy. Her head was square and small, like her body. This combination of unusual qualities in her face and figure increased her exotic and feminine appeal, and made her appear much younger than her years.

Her intense radiance compensated for the many years that drained her from her life force by the constant and heavy loss of menstrual blood. And like her fellow disciple, Ester, she had been rejected by those in her village. Consequently, she had never been married and, after these last two years of discipleship, she wasn't sure if she could possibly tolerate a marriage. Besides, she was forever an outcaste for traveling as a single woman, and for traveling in the company of men. It didn't matter that her virtue was physically intact, and that her spirit was pure. It didn't matter that the small cadre of unmarried sisters, who traveled with Jesus, kept within each other's company and usually stayed in pairs when dealing with their beloved brother disciples whether in private or in public. It didn't matter. This was not done. Men were not to speak to women in public; not even to their wives or sisters or mothers.

Such behavior caused a permanent stain. Such behavior was considered wanton. In fact, according to the mainstream of society, she and her sister disciples were classed below slaves and prostitutes and lepers and, therefore, were in no class at all.

Despite being shunned, she wore the customary mantle that covered her head, face, and upper body out of respect for her Master, out of simple modesty, and out of fear of intolerant and violent men who were unpredictable in their whimsy at enforcing the law—a disguise for their hatred of women. This alone, made her and her fellow sister disciples close to each other, especially when not within the immediate sphere of their beloved Jesus, who saw their virtue and beauty, and who expressed kindness and love to them all.

Jesus' extreme gentleness to them was unworldly, even though he was a man.

A man. No woman could fully trust a man. But this man, Jesus, Jesus, was truly a man for any woman.

This woman, she thought.

She'd been spoiled forever. She could not be a bride to anyone who behaved less than her gentle and strong and radical man called Jesus.

She realized the mantle was still in her hand, noted the terror in the eyes of her sister, who had remained at her side, then placed the mantle over her head like a scarf. She did not cover the lower portion of her face. "He loved the poor in us. He recognized our sacrifice."

"To be a woman is to sacrifice," her sister disciple said.

"He knew that."

"Men. They donate from their surplus."

"Selfish. Yes."

"We give from the poverty of ourselves."

"Yes, yes, dear sister. We give with our entire lives, with our wombs. We give everything."

"Oftentimes, our very lives."

"Everything, yes, everything."

"Our Lord has given with his life."

"Then . . . then that leaves us with . . . with what?"

"Nothing." She tugged at the loose ends of her mantle as she peered at Jesus. "Nothing is all that's left."

The ground trembled. Several crows flew over the murdered earth.

The other woman sought comfort with an embrace. "I'm frightened."

"So is our Lord. So is our Lord." Her words were delivered with the careful authority borne from the increase of alienation. She covered her face with her mantle.

"Eloi, Eloi, lema sabachthani?"

"The King of the Jews." She spat on the ground. "You mean, this madman said he was the King of the Jews."

❖

"Eloi, Eloi, lema sabachthani?"

The three notable circles of women drew closer together in support of Blessed Mother, who remained silent.

"*'Why have you forsaken me?'* Is that what he said?" asked Mary of Magdala. "Is that—"

"No," said Blessed Sister. "*'Why have you abandoned me? Abandoned me,'*" she emphasized nervously.

"*'Lema sabachthani?'* he said, *'lema sabachthani?'*" Peter's mother-in-law, Shelomith, interjected with authority at her sister disciples and at the weather. "*'Lema sabachthani?!'*" she emphasized with additional authority.

Disquiet spread quickly among these three tightly grouped sister disciples:

"You mean, *'Why did you discard me?'*"

"Wait. *'Why have you deserted me?'*"

"No! *'Neglected me,'* he said—"

"*'Relinquished me,'* you mean."

"*'Surrendered,'* I heard him say, *'surrendered me.'*"

This cacophony of disagreement continued nervously from the murmuring lips of these unsure sister disciples, who were trying to be sure of the unsure with words like: rejected me, abjured me, renounced me, forsworn me, disgorged me, betrayed me and me and me and me—

"Oh, God! Oh, God!" Mary of Magdala cried in response to their discord despite Blessed Mother's calm embrace. "Whatever he said, whatever—he is showing us how to die."

Hanna, the wife of Aaron, insisted on being heard by the tone of her expectant mother's voice. "Does he know where he is going? Does he? He spoke, I'm sure, he spoke to God."

"Yes. He did," said Mary. "And yet, he's dying in fear and pain and abandonment from himself."

"Even he?" Hanna probed.

"Yes. Yes," Mary insisted, feeling the strength of Blessed Mother's calm silence. "Because we . . . we all do. This does not contradict our trust in God. We . . . we can fear death, and still have faith that God is waiting for us after death."

"Like him," Salome proclaimed.

"Jesus." Hanna whispered. "He is . . . is—"

"Bigger than life. Bigger than himself." Mary looked to Blessed Mother for confirmation. "And yet, he is a man."

"*Eloi, Eloi, lema sabachthani?*" Blessed Sister whispered hopefully. "I think you're right, my sister. I . . . I think he does give us permission to die in dread and tears."

"It's about the blood." Hanna said with greater determination. "Follow the blood in death, as well as in life."

"In life, yes. In giving life: through the blood, and the pain of giving birth." Mary felt Blessed Mother's embrace tighten with approval. "This fear, even in childbirth, does not run counter to God's love, or run counter to our faith in God's presence."

A melodic concatenation resounded among them:

"In God's presence."

"Amen."

"In his death."

"Amen."

"In our death. Any death."

"Amen. Amen."

"Eloi, Eloi, lema sabachthani?"

The heavenly forces shook and brought terror and dismay among many of Golgotha's women, despite their faith and love and determination—all were shaken by their doubts, and by the portents in the sun and the wind and the earth.

The surrounding signs of oblivion prevented all hope for escape. Then again, escape to where? And from whom?

Solemn prayers and petitions could be heard in all directions. Prayers of terror. Prayers of hope. Prayers to combat the omens embodied in growling dogs nearby, cawing crows above, and laughing hyenas in the distance.

Dinah was impervious to the tumult of the natural and supernatural elements but not to the surrounding groups of high-strung women. Like a leper, Dinah stood alone: unclean in the eyes of many sister disciples, and unsightly among those in the other groups of women, who were camped before Jesus at distances in keeping with their politically earned social strata and feminine power.

Dinah surveyed Golgotha:

Jesus was not alone. Among invisible women, this Jesus was not alone. And neither was her beloved brute, Azriel.

Dinah suddenly felt contempt for their pettiness, felt contempt for their struggle over a dying man's love. Anger seized her. "You idiots! You hypocrites!"

She aroused Azriel from unconsciousness.

Azriel directed a vicious tirade against her. "You whore! Get away, I told you!"

Dinah ignored Azriel's foul address. "I'm here, my love."

Black stool oozed down the support peg that Azriel was perched upon. The rough gurgle of passing gas accompanied a foul odor. "Kiss my ass!"

"I'm not going!" Dinah countered.

"Whore! Bitch! Worthless woman!"

"I would have made you a good wife and mother."

"Barren whore!"

"I've sinned with you, yes. And I'll accept barrenness—"

"Get away, I said! You were nothing but pleasure to me!"

"I drew pleasure from you as well. As well."

Azriel sobbed.

"Darling. Darling. Listen." Dinah's voice softened as if she were singing a lullaby to a child at bedtime. "I wanted to have your child. I would have been a good wife to you. I would have ground the grain and baked your bread and laundered your clothes. I would have cooked and nursed your . . . your adopted children. I would have made your bed and—"

"Woman, woman, stop! You're killing what's left of me."

"Early in the morning I start the fire in the oven," she whispered. "Then warm your bread after drawing water from the well."

Azriel listened with increased calm, and with an increased escape from himself.

"I feed you and the children, and send you off to your labors refreshed. I nurse and watch the children while you are away. I sew and work in wool. I work for you."

Someone threw a stone aimed at Jesus, but hit Azriel instead.

"What. What! You scum!" Azriel slammed his head against the back of the stake in a madness intended to do harm to himself. "Get away, woman!"

Dinah picked up a stone. "Damn you!" She turned in the direction from where the stone had been thrown and searched for the guilty person. "Where are you? Where are you!? I'm going to kill you!"

"Shut up," one of the Roman guards commanded.

"I'm not afraid of you." As soon as she raised the stone to hurl it at the Roman guard, she felt a dull pain on the side of her neck and on top of her right shoulder, which radiated down the side of her body. She fell face down onto the ground, and almost lost consciousness. As soon as she turned her head and rested her left cheek on the muddy ground, she saw the heavy leather sandals of a Roman guard standing near her.

"This woman is as crazy as the man she stands before," said one of the guards.

"She's all right, Vespa," said the other guard that Dinah had threatened. "Leave her alone."

"I'll finish her if you want, Strabo."

"Leave her alone, you . . . you scum!" Azriel shouted.

Both guards laughed.

"What are you going to do, big man?" Vespa taunted.

"I'd break your backs if I were standing before you."

"See what I mean?" said Strabo. "I understand her better than these other women. At least she's defending a man."

"More man than either of you," Azriel shouted.

Strabo chuckled. "Besides, she amuses me. They both amuse me."

"Well, I don't like her," said Vespa, itching to employ some violence.

"I don't like any of them. But I dislike her, and him, the least. Leave her alone."

Vespa, who was still standing near Dinah, nudged her side with the bottom of his heavy sandal. "Your lucky day, missy. Strabo wants you to live. Throw your anger at your own kind." He nudged her side again. "Behave."

The guard walked away leaving Dinah semi-conscious and hurt but unafraid under Azriel's dying shadow.

"Eloi, Eloi, lema sabachthani?"

She stood at the foot of Nikos' cross. She was one of two women who took care of the already forgotten thieves, who were forced to accompany her Lord to this place of the skull to die. She stood at the foot of the young Greek's cross because he was alone, and because she knew Nikos had fallen in love with her on the main roadside that led to Golgotha. She realized after she wiped his face of blood and dirt, after she gave him wine to drink, after she spoke comfort to him, that he had never known tenderness in his life. He had to fall in love with her. He had to. And in so doing, she liked to think he reached out to her Lord for mercy because of her tenderness: her tenderness combined with her Lord's, who said to him, *"Tonight you will be with me in paradise."*

She was young, like Nikos, and possessed that handsome quality of youth, which transcended culture and class. She wore her mantle as a veil over a full-length tunic that was sleeveless, and loosely girded around her hips.

Beauty radiated through her compassionate eyes. Beauty emanated through the radiance of her countenance. Then there was beauty: thick black hair, heavy eyebrows, long lashes, full lips, earthy brown skin. And there was beauty: slender figure, graceful movements, uncritical demeanor.

She believed in the Messiah. She believed in his love. She believed in the life beyond, through him. She believed in the Kingdom of God. She believed Jesus saved Nikos, with her help.

✛

"Eloi, Eloi, lema sabachthani?"

Fourteen years old. Slight figure. Prominent facial features. Long black hair. Narrow hips. Virgin eyes.

As the ground shook and as the strange gloom fell upon the earth and as his words *Eloi, Eloi, lema sabachthani* kept rattling inside her skull, she wanted to vomit the darkness within her to caste out the remaining evil spirits that survived yesterday's light of Jesus' presence and forgiveness.

She spoke to Prisca, who stood beside her, in order to prevent the dark spirits from fully occupying her again. She was angry. "The man raped me. But all my father could think about was his bride price."

"Yes, yes, I know," said Prisca. "You've told me."

"When my father questioned me, there was doubt in his voice. Not concern about my feelings, or worry about my well-being. My own father! He doubted that the sexual violence against me was forced."

"Easy, Achsah." Prisca supported her sister by placing her right arm across Achsah's shoulders. "We are all in mourning for ourselves right now."

Achsah slumped against Prisca, her dearest sister disciple, who listened to Achsah's voice deepen as if someone else were speaking through her. Prisca trembled when Achsah went into a trance and her dark eyes lost focus.

"'Well, it happened in Jerusalem.'"

"And? And!?"

"'Well, you could have cried out.'"

"But I did, Father, I did!"

"'You should not have been so careless about your virginity.'"

"Excuse me?"

"'You should not have walked the streets alone, my careless daughter.'"

"I was getting water for the household. I was going to our nearby cistern!"

"'You'll have to marry him.'"

"I will not."

"'You are no longer a virgin. How am I going to find you a suitable husband now?'"

"You mean, how will you fetch a virgin price for a non-virgin on the marriage market?"

"'Don't be disrespectful. You are not alone in your suffering, my daughter. You are part of the family. This seducer—'"

"Rapist!"

"'Must make amends to me and your mother and your grandmother and—'"

"To everyone but me!"

"'How can you be so unreasonable?'"

"I was hurt! I was violated. I was taken away from myself. Don't you understand? He has killed me inside. Inside."

"'You'll mend.'"

Achsah exhaled bitterly. Tears streamed down her cheeks. She remained within her trance.

"'I'm sorry, Child. I . . . I'm simply trying to do what's best for you. What's done is done.'"

"I won't marry him."

"'He denies he violated you. And unless someone else saw you object—'"

"You mean another man."

"'Preferably, of course. But having been with another woman while seeing to your household duties would have made a difference.'"

"I will not marry that monster. He hurt me."

"'Then, my not-so-eligible daughter, you will have to stay home and live with this stain.'"

Achsah shook her head, then straightened her back as her trance dissipated.

Prisca dropped her supporting arm from Achsah's shoulders. "Your father certainly was shortsighted. But I believe that in time he would have spoken to you with greater understanding."

"My father had nothing more to say. We never spoke again. I never spoke to my mother again. I had lost everything, including myself. Then . . . then one day, I heard about this . . . this Messiah." She softened. "My Jesus. Even after second and third hearsay, his words had power. I decided I had nothing to lose. I knew he was my only escape. So I ran away and sought him and his wandering group of disciples. I was determined to find him and join his band, or die. I took what household money I could find in place of my dowry, packed a heavy burden of food and clothing, and set out into . . . into, what? The abyss. Yes. That's what it was, the abyss of uncertainty, of the unknown, of a woman alone, of a maiden without her father's blessings or her brother's protection—nothingness. The abyss meant death if I did not succeed in finding this Jesus I had heard about, if I did not succeed in touching his garment and somehow catch his attention from among the many." She pressed the palms of her hands against her heart. "I succeeded. And when he looked into my eyes, he saw through me and said: *'You are cleansed my child. Come with me.'*" She lowered both arms to her side. "And from that moment on, I was no longer the same person. From that moment on, I gave myself to him entirely. I discarded my whole life and distributed all that I had among his disciples, who embraced me and welcomed me as one of them." She spread her arms toward heaven. "By having nothing, I gained everything. By losing myself, I lost the darkness caused by that violent act inside of me." She sighed. "Jesus loves me. And I love him."

Prisca nodded.

Achsah inhaled deeply, then exhaled slowly. She was no longer angry. The surrounding darkness and the stillness in her Master's body no longer frightened her.

"Eloi, Eloi, lema sabachthani?"

Deep and gentle wailing persisted from all four points on the hill. Tears, mixed with the sky's downpour, supported the invisibility of the mourning women.

The murmur of grief from all directions eliminated any single source of irritation that the nervous Roman guards could act violently upon. Consequently, the Roman guards reasoned that, like the celestial bodies and the present storm, nothing could be done about Golgotha's women.

The darkness deepened with the increase of the rain's patter and with the furtiveness of the women's chatter. Death and time hung in the air.

"*My God, my God, why have you forsaken me?*'" an elderly woman from Galilee translated. Then she continued speaking as if she were reciting hidden knowledge, "*'Why are you so far from saving me, so far from the words of my groaning?*'"

"From where does that come, my sister?" asked a young woman who stood nearby.

"From within, my daughter. Deep within. And it has been written, *'Dogs have surrounded me. A band of evil men have encircled me. They have pierced my hands and my feet.*'"

"But he is . . . he is — what will we do now?"

"Have faith, my child."

"I'm cold and hungry."

"Overlook yourself, child. A single day's fast is nothing compared to the sacrifice of our famed prophetess, Anna, daughter of Phanuel."

"I know, I know," the young Galilean woman remarked with impatience, having heard about this eighty-four-year-old prophetess, widowed at an early age after seven years of marriage. "An angel among women—"

"Who publicly gave thanks to God, and spoke about the child," she gazed at Jesus, "about the Messiah, to all who waited for the deliverance of Jerusalem."

"Do you truly believe he is?"

"Don't you?"

"I've heard the story about this prophetess—"

"Anna."

"Yes. Anna. She was serving the Lord at the Court of Women one night—"

"She never left the temple grounds, it is said. Day and night for years and years, she fasted and prayed—"

"And, it is said, that she did more than speak about the child—"

"True, true—"

"It is said, she had a vision during the presentation of our . . . our Jesus, as a child being purified according to the Law of Moses, and that—"

"He was the Messiah, who had finally come to our people," the elderly Galilean declared.

"The Messiah. Do you really think—"

"Really. Must you think?"

"No. No. I suppose not. And . . ."

"And?"

"My dear prophetess: the earth is trembling."

"And, he is not dead."

"Father, into your hands I entrust my spirit."

A tired woman offered her breast to her ailing infant.

"Father, into your hands I entrust my spirit."

Even though her head was covered with a square of cloth, which was held in place with a length of fabric wrapped around her head, her thick black hair peeked out from both sides of her face. The heavy waterproof weave in her woolen tunic protected her young and strong body against the wet and the cold.

"Father, into your hands I entrust my spirit."

"That child needs swaddling."

"Who can afford it? The baby appears warm enough."

"A child can't be too warm under these conditions."

"Father, into your hands I entrust my spirit."

The boy wore a simple unbelted tunic and a small brimless cap. The girl standing beside him was similarly dressed, but her wild wet hair hung loosely over her shoulders.

"Father, into your hands I entrust my spirit."

The young Galilean woman embraced the elderly Galilean to seek comfort, even cold comfort and reassurance in support of her earlier words that he was not dead.

The elderly prophetess responded to the young Galilean's need by gently repeating his words, *"Father, into your hands I entrust my spirit.'"* Then continued in a whisper, *"'You have redeemed me, Oh Lord God of truth.'"*

"Lord, God. Truth. What is truth?"

The old woman stroked the girl's head. "There, there, my beauty. There."

"Father, into your hands I entrust my spirit."

John banged his forehead against the wood of Jesus' cross. He banged his forehead repeatedly. He banged his head.

Pain. Blood. Darkness.

"I am thirsty. It is finished."

"He is finished, he said, he is finished," said a large-breasted lady, who stood among the most devoted group of unknown women that followed Jesus from Galilee.

"My God, my God, he is dead. The son of Adam is dead," said another steadfast woman.

Unlike many who mourned and swayed and huddled against the terrible blanket of darkness that had descended upon their souls, these disciplined sisters, these sister disciples from Galilee closed ranks like a well-trained Roman cohort prepared for battle, as several of them uttered:

"He will rise again, he said. In three days."

"Three days."

"He is dead, but I can still hear his voice."

"His voice has always filled me with hope."

"With hope, his voice has filled my heart, and will continue to live."

"Yes, live. Live inside of me in three days, and in six days, and in nine days, and in all the days of my life and after."

"Amen, my sister. I feel drunk with this hope. He will be raised, I think. In me, and in you and in—"

"Oh, how I need to hear these words."

"His words, you mean."

"Speak. Speak. We must continue to speak to those who've never heard him."

"We will speak his good news. And so will the many sisters who stand here on Golgotha."

"Yes. He is not alone."

"We will be his witness."

"Even if men refuse to believe us."

"We will witness."

"Even if men say we utter nonsense."

"We will witness."

"We will witness."

"We will witness."

Many of them brought the lower portion of their mantles up to their mouths.

"Loyal women of Galilee, if you are ashamed to be his witness," said the large-breasted lady, "he will be ashamed of you."

All the Galilean women released their mantles from their faces as if they were dropping their armor before a mortal enemy. Several of them responded with great determination:

"I am not afraid, I'll say."

"I am not ashamed, I'll show."

"I am not thirsty, I'll pray."

A young woman stood near the outer darkness of Golgotha where the slope of the hill started downward in a gradual decline across the rocky formation that defined much of Golgotha's circumference. The torrent of water, which cascaded down the side of the hill, filled a labyrinth of channels that had been formed within the rocky landscape through centuries of climatic erosion. As the young woman shifted away from the tightly packed Daughters of Jerusalem, a misjudged sidestep toward the outer edge of the hill caused her to slip.

A strong hand emerged from the group and grabbed her upper left arm to prevent her from falling. "Steady, sister."

The young woman beat her breasts with her right fist to ease her palpitations. "Thank you. Thank you." She stared down into the outer darkness. "Looks like a flood." She slipped again but held onto her strong-handed sister. Then she stared at the more distinguished circles of women. "How come they get to stand so close to Blessed Mother?"

"They're shrewd."

The young woman sneered. "Every time I think about all the water I've carried to her—"

"That's what you get for counting."

"Look at you, standing beside me, trying to hide your own resentment."

"Your insults will get you nowhere."

"I'm there already."

"Then perhaps you won't mind if I step away from nowhere and improve the condition of your existence."

"Very good. Very political. You have it all down, neat and nice."

"I don't have anything."

"Hmm. I see."

The strong-handed disciple did not step away from the young woman.

They did not continue to speak or regard each other's presence. From a distance, they appeared to stand as sisters.

CHAPTER 9

Romans

Another kind of storm, more threatening and more violent, approached the hill and frightened away the last remnants of the riffraff, who were lurking in the outer darkness and hoping for easy pickings from those weakened by deep mourning. The approach of this masculine element, with its penchant for random violence and its disregard for pain and suffering, frightened the women of Golgotha.

"Get out of the way, you!" The man's voice was deep and violent and Latin.

Two women yelped.

Dissonant cries spread alarm and increased discord across Golgotha, shattering the consonant prayers that the sister disciples had managed to produce until now.

The squad of eight Roman Legionnaires, led by a calloused junior officer, marched in a two-by-two formation across the hill from Jerusalem's gate without altering the formation's course. The soldiers were eager to draw their swords and strike down anyone who obstructed their progress. Anybody in their way was either pushed aside or trampled.

A woman screamed. Another cursed.

Several babies began to cry as the Roman squad proceeded toward the executed criminals. Hardened to the last man, these veterans had seen their share of combat. Harsh winds and deprivation, brutality and death, rape and destruction had been familiar forces in their military lives. Rome's frontiers were constantly expanding and Rome's besieged empire was in constant need of protection, which placed a continuous burden upon Rome's Legions.

One of the auxiliaries standing guard near the brutish-looking criminal on the wood sneered at the approach of these regular-army legionnaires, who were equipped with better weapons, heavier armor, and superior provisions.

The mercenary, auxiliary legionnaires, who were regularly posted guards on Golgotha, were from Caesarea. Unlike the regular-army legionnaires, they and the other men in the cohort, who were garrisoned in Judea, were more tolerant of the people living in Jerusalem. Also, garrison life in Judea had eroded their discipline and encouraged them to take shortcuts in training. Consequently, auxiliaries tended to be lax while on post, as well as inconsistent in their treatment of the citizenry. In fact, the long-term occupation in Judea had reduced these well-trained auxiliary soldiers into petty garrison guards.

Like the approaching Roman squad, the auxiliaries wore leather helmets and articulated-plate body armor that covered the chest, shoulders, and back. Every other man in this Roman squad had a club swinging from a leather line tied to his dagger belt; their leather belts held long and short double-edged swords.

Unlike the large, curved, rectangular shields of their approaching legionary comrades, the auxiliary's round shield was smaller and inferior in quality, despite the fact that both kinds of protective equipment were made of strips of wood glued together, covered by leather, and secured with a bronze binding around its edge. This was heavy protection, which also became a burden after long hours of guard duty. Consequently, the shields were either set aside, or laid on the ground.

One of the guards leaned against his lance, which had an iron head with a sharp point to pierce his enemy's shield and a barb to prevent its removal. He adjusted his full-length cloak, which was wrapped closely around him and securely pinned at the neck and chest. A hard gust of wind tore at the loose lower end of his cloak and drove the slanted rain underneath the tightly woven, waterproofed garment. "Damn this strange weather, Strabo."

"Damn this edge of Rome's empire, Vespa."

"I hope that approaching squad is our relief."

"Don't be stupid. Those are regular legionnaires. Soldiers."

"Then what are they doing here?"

"We're about to find out. Straighten up, Vespa. Pick up your shield. There's an officer with them."

"I'm not afraid of that one."

"He can have a mean bite."

"Nah. He's hard up the ranks. He's been one of us." Vespa wrapped his full-length cloak more tightly around himself.

"I don't think so," Strabo cautioned. "He's not one of us anymore."

The squad looked like an unworldly creature with eight cloaks angled backward due to the wind and eight lances angled forward due to the creature's discipline and readiness to inflict harm against anything in its path. Marching in silent cadence emphasized the creature's refusal to alter its course.

One of the creature's feet stepped on a fallen woman's hand. She cried out as another cursed at the soldiers in defense of the injured sister; the dangerous creature remained indifferent.

At the junior officer's command, the squad came to a halt beside Vespa and Strabo—one of two pairs of guards on the hill. The junior officer approached Vespa straight on with a glare.

Vespa's eyes widened with alarm before he acknowledged the officer. "Sir!"

"Your shield!" The junior officer demanded.

Vespa glanced at his comrade, Strabo, who anticipated the officer's behavior and who did not offer him
sympathy. "Yes, sir."

"Who's in charge of this watch?"

"I am, sir," said Strabo.

"A soldier. At last." Vespa clambered to Strabo's
side with his lance and shield in proper form before
the junior officer addressed Strabo again. "This man
should know better, Strabo."

"Strange weather, sir. Strange women."

"All the more reason to be on your guard."

"Sir."

The junior officer glanced at the other pair of
guards who stood behind the large and brutish-
looking criminal on the wood. They had already hus-
tled for their shields and had straightened the angles
of their lances, as well as their bearings. "Better.
Much better." He nodded. "All right." The officer
studied the surrounding women who had remained
on Golgotha. "Yes. Strange women. All these women,
they . . . they make me nervous."

Strabo relaxed his bearing. "They're like vultures
circling in the sky."

"Can't you get rid of them?"

"How long have you been stationed in Palestine,
sir?"

Disgust washed across the officer's face. "Ahh.
Too long. One more day is too long." He turned to his
sergeant. "Let's get on with it, Sergeant."

"Yes, sir." The sergeant broke ranks and assigned
two men to each executed criminal.

"On with what, sir?"

"We're here to break these men's legs, Strabo."

"Now you're talking, sir," Vespa said, with relish. "But why?"

"Orders. Something to do with their Sabbath Laws. I don't know. I don't care. Orders."

Vespa grinned. "It's rare to hear orders that please me so much."

"Why?"

"To get us off this post."

"You're not going anywhere," said the junior officer.

Vespa was crestfallen. "I thought—"

"Once my detail is accomplished, you're to stay and preserve order here."

"But, sir. These women aren't doing anything. There is no disorder here."

"Then keep your sword in your scabbard and bear it!"

Vespa dared not press any further with this unbending junior officer. "Yes, sir."

The officer glanced at Strabo. "You need to straighten him out."

"Garrison guard duty is hard on auxiliary soldiers, sir."

The officer nodded with understanding, then— "Sergeant?"

"On our way, sir!"

"Very well." The officer noticed the approach of two men from the north side of the hill. "What have we got here?"

Strabo turned to look. "They seem pretty official to me, sir."

"Hmm. Wealthy Judeans. We'll see." The officer heard a man groan, sought its origin, and discovered John's crumbled figure at the foot of Jesus' cross. "And what's that?"

Vespa chuckled. "One of them gone mad, sir."

"Not sure, sir," Strabo qualified. "Pathetic creature though. The women seem to tolerate him."

The officer addressed his sergeant, again. "Get him out of here."

"Yes, sir." The sergeant turned to the unassigned legionnaire. "That one's yours."

The soldier nodded. "Sergeant." Then he warily approached John.

"Get on with it, Sergeant." The officer strolled a short distance away to separate himself from his working troops.

"The middle one is already dead, Sergeant," said Strabo.

"You mean, the King?"

"The what?"

"The placard nailed above his head."

"Oh. That. Can't read, Sergeant."

"Well, the King is dead." The sergeant turned to the pair of soldiers assigned to Jesus. "Use your lance on that one instead."

The soldier nearest Jesus pricked the King's left thigh with the point of his lance. "Strabo's right, Sergeant. This one's dead."

"Run him through anyway," said the Sergeant.

The dull thud of a club smashing against Azriel's thigh bone reverberated across Golgotha. The pair of guards assigned to Jesus, as well as the sergeant, turned their attention to the pair of guards assigned to the brute.

Azriel bawled in response to the blow; Dinah shouted foul invectives at the legionnaires; and John screamed when the legionnaire assigned to drive him away pricked him with the point of his lance, then kicked him.

Emotional chaos spread across Golgotha.

Veins of lightning etched across the sky and illuminated John's cowardice. He caressed the lower portion of the stake; the time for courage had past.

John was startled by a clap of thunder so intense, that he jerked forward and hit his head against the stake and, therefore, assisted the legionnaire in his work.

The legionnaire laughed cruelly.

John crumbled, face down, onto the muddy ground. He sobbed with self-loathing; the time for prayer had past.

In response to another kick from the Roman legionnaire, John brought his forearms down across his abdomen. The next kick forced him to roll away from the legionnaire's wrath. The numerous kicks that followed made him tumble down the hill, vomiting and spitting blood. At the bottom of the hill, John howled, then crawled into the outer darkness as quickly as he could, hoping the legionnaire wouldn't follow him. He thought he heard the shout of another

Roman legionnaire and the curse of a woman as the darkness of unconsciousness descended upon him.

Dinah stood before her Azriel, defying the pair of legionnaires assigned to the brutish thief. "Don't hit him again!"

"Get away woman, or you'll feel the pain of this club, as well!" The legionnaire brandished the wooden club at Dinah. "I said get away!"

"Haven't you done enough to him?" Dinah challenged. "Leave him alone, you Roman dog!"

One of the two legionnaires assigned to Azriel approached her with every intention of hurting her. "I have my orders."

Dinah stepped away from Azriel to avoid the legionnaire's club but continued to spit venomous language at him.

The legionnaire frowned at her with respect. "Stay where you are and you'll not be hurt."

"I'll take care of her," said the other legionnaire.

"Nah. She's got backbone. Leave her alone. Here. Hold my lance." The legionnaire turned to Azriel with his club firmly gripped in both hands. "I'm not sure his break is complete. I'll use both hands, this time."

The sound of the club striking Azriel a second time made Dinah fall to her hands and knees in tears. "Dogs. Dogs. Miserable, miserable dogs."

The second blow succeeded in shattering the large thighbone of Azriel's left leg. Azriel howled like an injured wolf in harmony with John's pathetic mongrel yowl from the distant outer darkness.

"What's that, Sergeant?" The legionnaire with the club peered in the direction of the agonized yelp.

"I think Gordo found that lunatic I assigned him to again." The Sergeant and the men of his squad laughed, along with Strabo and Vespa and the other pair of guards, who were posted near Azriel. "I guess he thought he could escape into the outer darkness to avoid further injury."

"Not from Gordo," said the soldier with the club.

John yelped and yowled with Azriel's continuous sobs.

Strabo nodded to convey his professional respect. "Go, Gordo."

"He likes his work," said the Sergeant.

"Hell," Vespa countered. "He's just pissed off, like me."

The sergeant looked toward the pair of soldiers assigned to Nikos just as one of them struck the Greek boy's right thigh. The sound of the break was unmistakable. There was no cry; Nikos was too deeply unconscious to respond.

"Hey, Sergeant, this one isn't very far from death."

"Good for him," said the Sergeant.

The junior officer, who had maintained his distance from his men's assigned duties, almost drew his short sword against the figure he discovered standing too close to him. "What the—" His sword remained half way in his scabbard when he saw that it was a beautiful expectant mother, a small and harmless woman. "What are you doing?" He pushed the exposed portion of his sword back into its scabbard. "What do you want?"

Hanna trembled before him. Her seven months could be seen.

"Speak up," the officer demanded. "Speak up, I said. Your beauty has saved you."

"Why are you breaking their legs?" she asked.

"Orders."

"Hanna!" Mara approached her from behind. "What are you doing?"

"But why?" Hanna persisted, ignoring Mara.

"Step away," said the officer. "I don't explain orders. Step away. For your own safety."

Mara tugged the back of Hanna's cloak. "Hanna, be careful."

"But I don't understand why—"

"Listen to your companion, beautiful lady. I don't want to lose my temper with you."

Hanna obeyed the restrained officer and accompanied Mara back into the safety of the other women. She whispered. "I don't understand why they must be so cruel."

"They're Romans," said Mara. "And I think I heard him say something about orders related to our Sabbath Law."

"Since when does a Roman care about our Laws?"

"Since Herod. Since . . . since our Lord. I don't know. Look!"

One of the two legionnaires assigned to the criminal King, finally pierced Jesus' right side with his lance. The legionnaire was startled by the intensity of the screams and the surge of the mourning by the surrounding women. He paused with the lance still impaled inside Jesus.

"What," said the other soldier assigned to Jesus. "Afraid of women, now?"

Vespa and Strabo, the other pair of guards, and several of the regular soldiers laughed.

"Their shrieks caught me off guard, that's all." The soldier pulled the lance out and quickly stepped aside from the explosive spurt of blood and water that shot out of the hole in Jesus' right side. "Whoa. Look at this. Their King tried to piss on me."

Laughter erupted among the soldiers and guards.

An increased mutter of prayer arose from the many women. Their huddles became tighter as the intensity of their words grew louder.

"Ahhhhh! Ahhhhh!" Azriel's broken body forced him to moan continuously.

Dinah scooped up a clod of mud and threw it at one group of women. The soldiers and guards watched with interest.

"Strabo, look."

"Shhh. Let's see what happens, Sergeant, let's see."

"Right. Right."

The men watched with eagerness.

"What good will that prayer-babble do for any of these men! You! Idiots!" Dinah scooped up more mud.

Hanna stepped toward her. "Throw more mud at us and you'll have to answer to me."

"Hanna!"

"Mara. Don't."

Mara was surprised by Hanna's rebuke. She remained where she stood, dumbfounded.

Caught in the middle of her intent, Dinah's arm remained extended behind her with the clod of mud dripping from her hand. She laughed when she realized that it was Hanna, the little pregnant woman, who challenged her. "You!? I can eat you alive."

"Don't. Don't do it."

Their eyes met and exchanged the intensity between them. Neither woman backed away. Neither woman was bluffing.

Dinah stepped toward Hanna, who stood her ground.

The prayer among the surrounding women intensified. Mara's astonishment grew. The soldiers and the guards wagered among themselves with an enthusiasm ordinarily found at the beginning of a cockfight.

The officer stepped between them. "I'll decide who will and will not fight." The soldiers and guards were visibly disappointed. The officer looked at Dinah. "Drop that mud." Then he peered at Hanna. "Step back." After both women obeyed, he studied Jesus on the cross. "This leader of yours: wasn't he a messenger of peace, or some such nonsense?"

"Nonsense, for sure," Dinah remarked. The wind and the rain veered.

"Ah, not a follower." The officer glanced at Hanna before addressing Dinah. "I see the reason for this conflict now. Good. Very good."

"What?" Dinah challenged. Azriel's continuous groaning tormented her.

"I understand one of you, at least." Then he addressed Hanna. "What do you expect from your leader now?"

"He . . . he is our Messiah."

The officer smiled. "Truly he was the son of God. Is that it?" He laughed behind his rhetorical question. "You Judeans and your God. Not healthy. Look where your God has taken your so-called Messiah. Look. Pathetic." He sneered at Hanna. "Go back to your companions." He noted Mara. "Take control of her before I lose my temper." Mara approached Hanna. "Go, I said." He waited until Hanna and Mara joined the other women, then turned to Dinah. "And you. Shut up."

Dinah pointed at Hanna's group. "Then tell them to stop tormenting my man with their idiotic gibberish."

"I said, shut up!" The officer glanced at one of his soldiers, who approached Dinah, prepared to do her harm if so ordered. "Your man is dying over there. Go to him and be silent, or suffer the consequences."

Dinah glanced at the legionnaire, whose hard eyes possessed no compassion or mercy. She shrank from both men and approached Azriel, who was finally unconscious. She knelt before him, but offered no prayers.

The officer took active charge of his men again. "Sergeant!"

"Sir!"

"We've had enough amusement."

"Sir."

"Form the squad."

"Sir."

The officer strode toward Strabo as his squad mustered into formation. "Damn this strange weather. And damn these people."

"I can't tell one from the other," said Strabo.

"Who'd want to? Judeans. Galileans. Nazarenes. Bah! All the same. I'll be glad to leave Palestine." The officer noted the two men still standing close to the outer darkness. "And what's with those two Judeans?"

"I don't know, sir."

"You know what to do if they become a nuisance."

"Sir."

As soon as the soldiers took their places in the two-by-two column, the Sergeant stepped into the left position at the head of the squad. "All present and accounted for, sir!"

"Very well." The junior officer waited for Vespa to assume his station beside Strabo. "Are you sure the four of you will be able to handle this guard?"

Vespa sneered before Strabo could answer. "Against these women? Of course!"

The officer scowled at Vespa. "I wasn't speaking to you."

"Sir!"

"You'll taste the end of a flagrum if you forget to address me properly again."

"Yes, sir! Yes, sir!"

Strabo defended him. "It's been a long and strange day, sir." He peered at the strange darkness above. "Still is."

The officer nodded. "I understand, Strabo. But straighten him out." He grimaced at Vespa. "Or I will."

Vespa stiffened. "Sir."

"Hmm. Palestine. This place will be Rome's undoing." The officer positioned himself beside his squad, then turned to the sergeant. "To the gate!"

"Sir! F-o-r-ward—huuh!"

The creature marched across Golgotha, prepared to trample anybody in its way.

Vespa exhaled a breathy whistle. "What a hard ass."

"I told you."

"You'd have thought he was the only one who didn't like Palestine."

"Yeah, well, you'd better learn to keep your mouth shut, Vespa."

"Yeah. Well."

One of the other two guards approached Strabo and Vespa. "What was that all about?"

"You saw for yourself, Facilis," said Strabo.

"Yeah," Vespa added resentfully. "You managed to stay out of it nicely."

"I'm not stupid where it comes to officers. You need to keep your mouth shut. Right, Strabo?"

"I've told him."

"You're lucky you had Strabo beside you or that officer would have given you a taste of the lash."

"You think so?" said Vespa.

Facilis shook his head. "I know so."

"Next time, I won't pull him out of the fire," said Strabo.

"I didn't do anything."

Facilis chuckled, as he sauntered back to his post beside the other guard. "You've got your hands full, Strabo. I hope you don't feel the lash on his account."

"I won't, Facilis."

"Oh yeah," Vespa interjected. "Blame me for everything. Blame me—"

"And if I do, my friend, you won't be able to complain again."

Vespa blanched before the old veteran, who was capable of carrying out his threat. "I'm sorry, Strabo. Damn. I'm sorry."

Joseph of Arimathea and Nicodemus finally stirred from the edge of Golgotha's outer darkness. They started to approach Strabo and Vespa after the Roman squad departed, but hesitated, then stopped.

Vespa was the first of the two to catch sight of their movement. "Strabo, look at that. Those two are trying to gather enough courage to approach us. A couple of live ones, it looks to me."

"Easy," said Strabo. "They might have influence."

"You think so?"

"I'm not going to take any chances, right now. Not on this day. Let's wait and see what they do." Strabo peered at Vespa. "And if they do approach, you'll have an opportunity to prove yourself with me."

"Right. Right. I won't let you down."

"Hmm."

They waited for Joseph of Arimathea and Nicodemus to approach them.

CHAPTER 10

Brothers

The wind whipped and veered ferociously around Joseph of Arimathea and Nicodemus.

Joseph raised his mantle over his brimless hat, then threw the right end of the mantle over his shoulder to protect the lower portion of his face. He shuddered. "What do you think, my friend?"

"Those Roman guards look pretty hardened to me," said Nicodemus. He noticed Joseph's raised mantle. "Are you all right?"

"These old bones of mine, combined with the intensity of this season's 'latter rain,' have weakened me. Dear, God. What strange weather. And you're right. Those guards appear to be unpredictable."

Nicodemus surveyed the circumference of the horizon like a sailor gauging the weather. "These are not westerly winds from the sea. These . . . these circular winds seem to come simultaneously from the four quarters of the earth and the heavens."

"Like Rome's might and ferocity," said Joseph. "Unnatural. These winds are unnatural."

"God's breath, nonetheless."

"God. Yes. Oh, God, have mercy on this poor, old wrong-doer." The wind gusted. "Please blow away my desperateness and replace it with courage."

"The wind is . . . is HIS bidding." Nicodemus pulled his cloak more tightly around himself.

"What does all this mean? His death. His . . . his . . ."

"What does anything mean, anymore?"

Joseph sighed. "We should know better than to ask such questions."

"If we did not, we wouldn't be here: contrary to the council's wishes; among questionable women; at risk of losing everything."

"As well as our lives at the hands of those heartless garrison guards standing near our Master."

"I wonder," said Nicodemus, as if he had not heard Joseph's last remark.

"What?"

"Would I have dared to utter such a statement in his presence?"

"You mean, what does anything mean anymore? Hmm." Nicodemus nodded, gravely. "Such was his power."

"Yes. And where is it now?"

"We're here, aren't we?" Nicodemus frowned. "Aren't we?"

"Don't be offended, my brother."

"But . . . but there's got to be some power in that. There's got to be."

"I hope so, dear friend. I hope so." Joseph studied the Roman guards. "But I haven't completed my task, yet."

"You mean, we still haven't claimed our Lord's body."

"I don't know about you, but my knees are shaking."

"Only your knees? My body and soul tremble, dear friend. My body and soul."

"Please," said Joseph, "let's stand here a moment longer. Just a moment."

Joseph's stern and sallow countenance accentuated his age, disclosed his growing illness, and emphasized his intelligence. A full and well-groomed beard and mustache deepened his dark eyes that were set close above his distinguished nose. His expensively embroidered hat called attention to his membership in the High Council, his prosperity, his privilege, his position: above the common man, though teaching among them.

He wore two luxurious tunics: a long outer garment and a short one underneath. Draped over his shoulders was a richly dyed cloak made of tightly woven wool. Because his brimless hat ordinarily provided adequate protection from the elements, his mantle frequently hung from his neck like a scarf until he needed additional protection from the weather, needed to conceal agitation, or wanted to convey disapproval.

Nicodemus sighed. "We must confront those men."

"Easy for you to say. I'm still recovering from Pilate's glare."

Nicodemus threw a doubtful glance at Joseph. "Then I'll lead the way. I'm understood by most people. I can speak their language."

"Those are still Roman guards over there, even though they're from Caesarea. And these women—"

"You're right. I don't see any tolerance in that pair. But, they're men, like us. And we have authority and influence."

"That's one method of securing courage."

"I'm not denying my fear."

"And what about these women?"

"What about them?"

"Lately I've observed that this so-called authority of ours has been met with contempt by them."

"I . . . I haven't considered them." Nicodemus studied the women on Golgotha. "Since when do you need the approval of women?"

"You know as well as I do that Jesus changed their . . . their perceptions and their . . . their status among us."

"You mean, among his disciples."

"I mean, among those who saw, who cared, who . . . who trusted."

"Well, I'm . . . I'm trusted."

"Don't be offended, my friend. I'm not questioning your integrity, or your abilities."

"I see. I care," Nicodemus said defensively. "I know how to clarify the Law."

"And you interpret the Law well."

"But?"

"But you often forget to raise your eyes from the scrolls and seek meaning elsewhere."

"Now you're insinuating that I'm acting like a priest," Nicodemus countered, indignantly.

"I didn't say that. Don't get angry. What . . . what I mean is . . . is our Master—you do admit—"

"Yes, yes, our Master. I wouldn't be here with you right now if I hadn't already acknowledged him as our Messiah."

"Right. A Messiah who spoke as a Pharisee."

"Yes, yes. He supported the oral tradition."

"And who indirectly spoke in support of our fundamentalist brethren when he said he was not here to destroy the written Law."

Nicodemus shook his head. "He often confused me."

"Yes, yes. He spoke from many directions that seemed contradictory."

"Many. Many. And often, I did not understand him."

"Perhaps, we never will."

"Hmm. I hope we won't be too misunderstood."

Nicodemus wore an ornate headdress, which had been fashioned to resemble a nomad's turban, even though he had never ridden a camel and had never tended sheep. The expensive white linen head-cloth was bound to the head by a thickly braided cord made of colorful linen that was pulled down across the forehead and adjusted to the proper level at the back of his head. Giving the impression that he was like the common man was so politically important to Nicodemus that he ignored the contradiction.

In direct contrast to Joseph, his stoic colleague, Nicodemus' expressions were animated and his temperament was passionate. He spoke with his hands, sang out his words, shouted his anger, and performed his prayers.

His cloak was colorful and his outer tunic was flamboyant, not because he was wealthy, but because he enjoyed dressing youthfully, fashionably, and with some sense of gaiety. He ignored the disapproving attitude from his fellow council members. He did not care if they did not like the boldness of his tunic's stripes or the fastidious grooming of his beard, as long as they respected his knowledge of the Law, his position in the Sanhedrin, and his authority among them.

"Have you gathered enough courage?" Nicodemus finally asked.

"No. Have you?"

"No."

"Still. I must proceed," said Joseph, "Pilate's glare or not."

They walked further into the light of the wind-harassed oil lamps and torches, and toward the uncertainty of Rome's reception—a pair of brutish guards standing near Jesus' crucified body.

Several wailing women startled them. A woman's screech frightened them both to a standstill.

"These women," said Nicodemus. "They're out of control."

"Where are their men?"

"Shh, be careful," Nicodemus whispered. "One of these ladies might take off your head if you're heard saying that."

"Preposterous."

"Metaphorically speaking, of course."

"Bah. No metaphor can hide the facts. Where are his disciples?"

"Frightened by his loss. Like us." Nicodemus peered over his shoulder. "I'm warning you. These women—"

"Look. We're here," Joseph said, too righteously.

"Ahhh. That's because you and I have been listening to him in secret."

"You may have gone to him in the night, but—"

"You have shrouded your interest in a darkness even greater than mine."

"How so?"

"In self-deception," Nicodemus said flatly.

"Ahh." Joseph's face hardened with resentment. "We are who we are. We can't change overnight."

"Yes, yes, yes." Nicodemus smiled triumphantly. "Even into this day, you pretend to be less than what you believe about Jesus."

"You're a good one to talk about pretending. Every time I consider your headdress—"

"That's different. I . . . I pretend nothing."

"Ha." Joseph smirked. "Like I said, I'm here."

"Safe among these women," Nicodemus persisted. "Safe as an unknown follower to the general public. Like me. I admit. Like me." His left eye twitched. "What kind of bravery are we talking about?"

"I stood before Pilate."

"We've all done that many times as High Council members. Pilate knows you by name."

Joseph pouted. "I requested his body."

"Politics. Pilate has to appear to be making an effort at governing us once in a while."

"His sword is always at the ready."

"You're defending your brave act too relentlessly, my brother."

"Meaning what?"

"Nothing. Nothing." Nicodemus sighed. "Look. I know Pilate often disguises his power, which makes him more dangerous."

"Precisely."

"But not necessarily to you. Or me."

"Then who?"

"To the powerless."

"We are powerless, as well."

"You and I are not being hunted. That's why His . . . His disciples aren't here. They are afraid they are being hunted."

"But, but John stood before his cross."

"Stood?"

"He . . . he was there—"

"Briefly. As a madman."

"But our Master entrusted him with his own mother. You heard that yourself."

"Our Master was instructing him to the last."

"He should have cast out John's demons, instead."

"John should not have behaved as a madman." Nicodemus prevented his colleague from interrupting him. "As a madman. Romans do not see madness as a threat. Therefore, those guards were not concerned with him. You see, he and his madness made him silent—"

"I see. And, therefore, invisible—"

"That's right, my friend. As invisible as these women."

"That is, until he finally irritated that Roman officer."

"Well. Yes. He's still a man."

Joseph meshed the fingers of his hands together into a large fist and pressed the knuckles of his forefingers against his bearded chin. "The poor creature."

"Yes. Poor all of us."

"I suppose we should not allow our debate to conceal our cowardice any longer, and prevent us from doing what we must do."

"Yes. Well said. Let's do what we must do."

Joseph of Arimathea and Nicodemus made their final approach toward Jesus, and presented themselves before two Roman guards.

Strabo lowered his lance at an angle but did not fully present its iron point. "That's far enough, you two. What business do you have here among your women?"

Joseph ignored the insult. He bowed his head. "Sir. May I have a word with you?"

"What do you want?" Strabo repeated. "And what took you two so long to approach us?" he added cruelly, to destroy whatever measure of confidence that Joseph and Nicodemus may have managed to gather between them. "Even these women have shown greater courage than either of you."

Joseph's lips trembled. He avoided looking at Nicodemus for fear of losing what courage he had left. "We are here to claim this man's body."

"Which man?" Strabo demanded impatiently. "The King?"

Joseph bit his lower lip. "Yes."

"By what authority?"

"Pilate's."

Strabo glanced at Vespa. "I told you." He settled his gaze upon Joseph again. "Our officer has just left. He's the one who makes the decisions." Strabo straightened his lance. "Pretty convenient of you to have waited for him to depart."

"We . . . I didn't know."

"No matter," said Strabo. "I need written orders." He caught Vespa's addled expression and almost laughed; neither one of them could read.

Joseph reached inside his tunic. "I have Pilate's seal right here." Joseph presented the small document to Strabo.

Vespa snatched it from Joseph's hand. "Let me see that."

Strabo suppressed his laughter by casting his stern eyes upon Joseph. "Stand back. Go on."

Joseph and Nicodemus backed away several steps as both guards strode to the other side of Jesus' cross.

Vespa offered Strabo the document, then whispered. "What does this say? I can't read."

"Don't ask me. You know I can't read either."

Both men tried to decipher the symbols written on the folded document with Pilate's seal upon it.

"Hmm. I recognize the seal."

Strabo glanced at Vespa skeptically. "Is that his seal? How would you know his personal seal?"

"It looks pretty official to me."

"You idiot. Why do I continue to keep watch over you?"

"I'm sorry. I thought—"

"You thought, you thought. You're sorry, all right." Strabo brought the document closer to his eyes and studied the writing with great attention, while Vespa peered over his shoulder to see what those two Judean elders were doing.

Nicodemus nudged Joseph, then whispered. "That seal is not a forgery, I hope."

"Of course not. I took my chances with Pilate himself."

"So. Your story was true."

"Of course," Joseph whispered, straining to suppress his indignity.

"Then you truly have more courage than I do."

"Did you really think I made up that story about standing before Pilate?"

"I did have my doubts."

"But I thought you trusted my integrity."

"It's your turn not to be offended, my brother."

Joseph nodded, grudgingly. "Fine. Fine."

"It did take courage."

"Yes. Well." Joseph shrugged his shoulders. "What use is position and wealth if a man can't use his power when he finds it most important."

"Yes, yes. So. Tell me exactly what happened with Pilate?"

"There's nothing extraordinary to tell." Joseph kept a careful watch on the two guards. "I simply approached Pilate as a respected member of the Sanhedrin, and waited for him to consult with Herod. To my surprise, Pilate gave me his sealed written permission to claim our Master's body. He even conveyed Herod's sentiments to me."

"Herod with sentiment? And Pilate acting as his messenger?" Nicodemus fumed. "That political scoundrel. That monster. That—"

"Shhh, Nicodemus. Careful."

"There's nobody here."

Joseph surveyed the women. "Hmm."

"Anyway, this counterfeit sentiment. What was it?"

Joseph stepped closer to Nicodemus while maintaining a careful watch on the guards before whispering. "Herod said, *'Brother Pilate, even if no one had asked for him, we would have buried him, since the*

Sabbath is drawing near. For it is written in the Law, the sun must not set upon one who has been executed.'"

"Why would Herod care about the burial of a criminal before this Passover's Sabbath? Why?"

"I don't know. Except, perhaps—" Joseph looked at all three crucified men. "As you suggested, our Master is politically dangerous to Pilate and Herod and, as you well know, to our High Priest, Caiaphas. Believe me, they're leaving the criminals on either side of him to rot on the wood through this Passover's Sabbath and through all the Sabbaths beyond."

"He feared our Master, then."

"No. He fears him still."

"Yes. Yes."

"And you," said Joseph. "You, a rabbi, who pretends to be a common nomad with that headdress of yours. Why have you broken ranks with our High Court brethren? Why?"

"Because . . . because as you already know, one night I came to him, disturbed by my dreams."

"You've never shared the details of that night with me."

Nicodemus bowed his head. "I disturbed him from his slumber."

"He was already asleep?"

"Yes. But he was not annoyed. In fact, he told the others in the household, where he was staying, to go back to sleep. That I was his friend. Me. His friend."

"And then?" Joseph glanced at the preoccupied Roman guards.

"He led me to a room in the back of the household and had me sit with him." Nicodemus smiled. "I remember the ground was cool. I remember his encouraging silence. He waited a long time. He waited until I said, *'Rabbi. Rabbi, I know that you're a teacher sent by God. After all, nobody could do the incredible works that you do unless God is with him.'"*

"You said that to him?" Joseph was astonished. His involuntary animation made him self-conscious. He peered at the guards to see if they had noticed him.

"Yes."

"And?"

"And he said, *'Amen, amen, I swear to God, no one can enter the Kingdom of God without being reborn from water, and from the spirit above.'"*

"What does that mean?" Joseph demanded.

"Not exactly my question to him. But it carried the same spirit."

"Which was?"

"*'How can an adult be reborn?'* I asked him. *'Can you reenter your mother's womb and be born a second time?'* And he answered, *'Amen, amen, I tell you the truth, no one can enter the Kingdom of God without being born of water and spirit. What is born of the flesh is flesh, but what is born of the spiritual realm is spirit. So don't be surprised when I tell you that every one of you must be reborn from above. The spirit blows wherever it wishes. Like the wind, you hear the sound the wind makes, but you do not know where it comes from or where it's going. It is the same way with everyone reborn of the spirit.'"*

"How can that be possible?" said Joseph.

"That was my question, exactly."

"So, what was his answer?"

Nicodemus seemed embarrassed, then proceeded. "He said, *'You are a rabbi of Israel, and you don't understand this? I tell you the truth before God, we speak of what we know, and we testify about what we know, but none of you listen to the testimony of our message.'"* Nicodemus searched his memory for accuracy. "*'If you don't believe me when I tell you about the earthly things, how will you ever believe me when I tell you about the heavenly things? No one has ascended to heaven except the Son of Man, the one who descended from heaven.'"*

"I . . . I see." Joseph frowned. "Help me to understand this."

"I can only tell you what he said."

"Then tell me more. Quickly. Before those two idiot guards finally come to a decision."

Nicodemus inhaled, then exhaled. "He said, *'In the desert, Moses lifted the bronze snake on his staff, in the same way the Son of Man is destined to be lifted up. So, everyone who believes in him can have eternal life.'"*

"What other kind of life is there?"

"Shhh. I'm trying to remember. Let me see. This . . . *'this is how much God loved the world. God gave his only son, so that everyone who believes in him may not die but have eternal life. After all, God sent his son into this world not to be its judge but to save the world through him.'"* Nicodemus began to rush his words. *"'Those who believe in the son will not be judged. Those who don't believe in the son are already judged because they don't believe in God's only son. This is how the judgment works: light has come into the world, but people love darkness instead of light because people do evil things. All those who do evil things hate the light and will not come into the light because they are afraid that their deeds will be exposed. But whoever does what is true, will come into the light so that the truth of their deeds will become evident, and show that their deeds had been performed in God.'"*

"He told you all that?"

"Yes."

Joseph pulled his cloak more tightly around him as if in response to the weather, but it was in response to an internal shiver. "I confess, Nicodemus, that is more than I can digest at one time."

"I know. I felt the same way, at first."

"And then?"

"His words gradually unfolded within me."

"A glimmer," said Joseph. "Shine a little light on your understanding with me."

"Well." Nicodemus licked his lips. "I believe he meant, mind you, these are my thoughts, my interpretations—"

"Yes, yes, go on," Joseph whispered. "Those guards can't be much longer."

"Well. Let me see. I always had great respect for the Rabbi of Galilee."

"Our Lord Jesus, yes, yes, go on. Those guards are about to come to a decision."

"Then let me explain this without interruption, please."

"Sorry. Sorry."

"All right. Let me see. I've always lived by the sternest of religious rules."

"Yes, yes, so have I," added Joseph.

"Always sincere in my quest for the truth."

"For heaven's sake, Nicodemus."

"Stop rushing me."

Joseph's exasperation intensified. "All right!" He cupped his right hand over his mouth, afraid he had spoken too loudly.

"I visited him at night not because I was afraid—"

"You don't have to convince me of that," Joseph countered.

"I . . . I was not afraid to be seen with Jesus."

"Sure, sure, I understand." Joseph was near the end of his patience.

"I simply wanted to have a one to one conversation with . . . with the new Rabbi who . . . who came from God."

"His meaning, Nicodemus, please, his meaning."

"Sorry."

"Agh. Too late. Here they come."

The surly guards swaggered toward Joseph and Nicodemus to display their authority, as well as to conceal their illiteracy and uncertainty over the authenticity of the document.

"You two," said Strabo. "Over here."

Joseph responded to their command first. Nicodemus quickly followed.

"Pharisees, right?" Vespa qualified.

"Yes. And in the Council of Seventy," said Joseph.

Strabo nudged Vespa. "Sanhedrin. I told you." He handed the sealed order back to Joseph. "Only a fool would risk his life for the body of a criminal. Legitimate. You must be legitimate. Take the body."

"But disturb nothing else," Vespa warned.

"Right," Strabo emphasized. "Your King is all you leave with."

Joseph remained steady against Strabo's glare. "Thank you."

"Then get it done," said Strabo.

Nicodemus and Joseph stepped toward Jesus.

"Stay here," said Joseph, "while I fetch the servants who are camped not far from here. I'll be right back."

"You'll do no such thing," said Ester.

"Excuse me?" Joseph peered at her as if she were an insect.

"We are not that invisible," Ester said.

"Out of the way, woman. I have important work to do."

"Too late!" said Gath, an old slave woman, in support of Ester. "You, and you, are too late."

Nicodemus was the first to shrink away from the old woman. "Who are you?"

"I saw you, Pharisee." Gath pointed her right boney forefinger at Joseph. "And you, too." Gath turned to Ester and Tamar. "They are of the seventy who pressed the Law and encouraged Herod and Pilate to do their will against Jesus."

"I tried to defend him," Joseph countered.

"Weak. Weak!" Gath declared. "I heard everything as I tended the fire and kept watch at the door nearby. I listened carefully." She shook her head to emphasize her disapproval. "Men. Even one of his closest disciples denied him three times. One of those times was with me. Me! So don't squawk about your defense of him. Nothing. I hear nothing except defense of yourself."

Nicodemus stepped toward the defiant women. "I've come here to help give him a proper burial. His body will want for nothing." He pressed the palm of his right hand against his chest. "The best linen and spices from me." He pointed his right hand at Joseph. "A freshly cut tomb from him. And a bier with—"

"Too late," said Tamar, who stood beside Ester. "He was of the living. Not the dead! Ask any woman here. The living is what we are about. Birth. Birth!"

The old slave woman cackled in support of Tamar's defiance against these impotent men.

"Ladies, please, be reasonable," said Joseph. "We were the ones who were sympathetic toward Rabbi Jesus."

"I heard your High Priest ask him if he was the Anointed," said Gath, "the Son of the blessed God."

"I know, I know," Joseph countered. "'*I am*.' He said it." Joseph disliked the scrutiny of feminine eyes. "Never mind what else he said. '*I am*' was the blasphemy that Caiaphas sought."

"The blasphemy that damned him," Nicodemus added, "and prevented either of us from saying anything more in his defense."

"You were afraid," Gath declared.

"Of course we were," said Joseph.

"How could we have done anything more after that?" Nicodemus insisted.

"You cowards!" Ester shouted, then proclaimed to her sisters, "They're no different from the rest of our men. Look around. Where are they still?"

"We are here," said Joseph.

"Too late! Too late!" Tamar shouted. "Like my old sister just said: where were you when your High Priest and your, your fellow members of the council interrogated Jesus about his teachings and about his disciples?"

"I've told you, we did our best," said Nicodemus.

Gath turned to Ester. "Mind you, our Jesus betrayed nobody. He did not give the Sanhedrin any names. He was not an informer. He was a man." The old slave woman addressed Joseph. "And what are you?"

"A seeker of truth in the Law."

Gath spat at the ground in front of him. "What is the truth? You know nothing of the Law. Except to hide behind words, words, words."

"We tried." Joseph's increasing timidity alarmed Nicodemus.

"They—you and they—shuffled our Master through the night from place to place until you heard what you needed to hear in order to have him condemned."

"Woman, you were not fully there!" Nicodemus asserted.

Gath appealed to her sisters. "Who are you going to believe? Me? Or this . . . this, these repentant Pharisees. These two secret disciples who claim to have tried. These—"

Mary of Magdala, who had stepped away from Blessed Mother and Blessed Sister, placed a gentle hand upon Gath's right shoulder. "Calm yourself, my dear. You've succeeded. We understand."

The old slave woman's eyes filled with tears, but tears did not roll down her wrinkled cheeks. "Do you. Do you?"

"Yes." Mary glanced at Nicodemus and Joseph. "But these men are here to help us. Late as they are. Flawed as they are. Remember." She looked up at Jesus, then lowered her gaze to Gath's watery eyes. "Our Master was a teacher of forgiveness." She hugged the old sister. "What is the truth in any of us? We have all failed him in some way."

Gath nodded. Tears flowed down her wrinkled cheeks.

Nicodemus and Joseph bowed their heads in shame.

Mary of Magdala addressed both Pharisees. "Atonement will not come as easy as providing linen and spices, and a tomb. Oh no. Like the rest of us, you will have to look elsewhere for that."

"Forgive me," said Nicodemus, as he stepped closer to her. Then he sought Blessed Mother's attention. "And to you most of all, Mother of our Lord, I humbly ask for your forgiveness."

Blessed Mother illuminated her silence with a compassionate smile, then sought solace from her sister. Through a terse hand gesture and a serious twist in her lips, Blessed Sister summoned Mary to assist her with Blessed Mother.

Nicodemus felt empty.

Ester sought Joseph's attention with her eyes, then whispered. "We will take over the care of our Master from this moment on. With your assistance."

Nicodemus started to protest.

"Yes," Joseph said, more to Nicodemus than to Ester. "I understand. Things have changed. Must change." Joseph sighed, then whispered. "But I think nothing will truly change between men and women."

"That doesn't matter," Ester said. "Today is all that counts." She looked up at Jesus. "He's ours. Ours. And we will take him to his rest."

"All right. All right." Joseph motioned the other women to join him and Ester.

Ester beckoned Tamar. "Take care of Gath."

"I'll be all right," said the old slave woman. "I'm as strong as any of you."

Tamar took Gath by the upper arm. "Stand by me. It is I who needs your strength."

Gath winked at Tamar. "You big ones always need the most help." Her broken teeth appeared when she smiled at Tamar, then at Ester. "We are with you, Ester—you brave dear."

Ester ignored the praise and accompanied Joseph and Nicodemus. Together they approached the foot of

Jesus' cross as the other women watched with intense interest.

"Well. What now?" said Nicodemus.

They scrutinized the means by which Jesus was held in place on the wood.

Joseph nibbled on his lower lip. "I don't want to pull his wrists and ankles past the heads of those iron spikes."

Nicodemus reached inside his outer tunic and pulled out a metal object from the void above the belt wrapped around his waist. "This stone cutter's tool should help release him. See?"

"What in the world are you doing with that?" said Joseph.

"I know something of the crafts. I've watched them work." He presented the object to Joseph and Ester. "See? This iron chisel has a very sharp blade. A good solid rap on the head with that heavy hammer over there in that box, which I'm certain was used to nail our Master to the wood, can now be used to release him from his cross." Nicodemus went to the box and lifted the hammer out. He demonstrated the hammer hitting the head of the chisel. "See? A solid strike with this hammer against the chisel should shear the nail at the surface of the wood."

"Hmm. It'll take more than one blow," said Ester. "I've been much closer to the crafts than either one of you. Those spikes are iron, not bronze."

"Iron. Not bronze," repeated Joseph. "Dear, dear. Well. However many blows it takes."

"I don't want him mutilated anymore than he is," said Ester.

"Of course not," said Nicodemus.

Ester extended her hand to him. "Here. Let me do it."

"No." Nicodemus was determined to protect whatever pride he had left. "I'll not budge on this point. My shame is enormous as it is. I'll not let it grow any further."

Ester nodded. "Fair enough. We will work together."

"Right."

"I'll help hold his limbs in place," said Ester.

"I'll help support the body," Gath interjected.

"And I'll swing that hammer, as well," Joseph said, with a determination equal to Nicodemus' concern for his pride.

"We'll need ladders," Gath declared.

"We'll need several," said Joseph.

"There. Over there. Join me." Gath did not wait for him.

"Right." Joseph hesitated. "Right." He stole a glance at Nicodemus. "This will take some getting use to."

"There's no time for that," Ester countered. "Get over it."

Nicodemus shrugged his shoulders. "Unprecedented."

Joseph relented. "She's right."

"Besides, no one will remember." Ester discarded her cynicism. She summoned Tamar, as well as several other women. "Give us a hand."

Joseph scowled. "My God. More women!"

"Do you see any men around here who would care to remember your . . . your affiliation with us?" Ester taunted.

Joseph scanned Golgotha. "No. Only the guards. And, if there are any other men who—well, they would be lurking in the outer darkness and . . . and, therefore—"

"Precisely," Ester interrupted.

Joseph exhaled. "Then, call more women."

Ester smiled. "I don't have to call again. Look. They're here."

"Do they know what to do?"

"We've tended to our Master's needs all along. We'll tend to him now, as well."

Abatal, the tall Samaritan woman and a ready volunteer, spoke up. "I've been a good wife. To all my husbands. I have ground the grain, baked, and laundered. I have cooked and nursed my children. I have made the beds and worked in wool. I am also a Samaritan, as you can see by my dress. But if you'll permit me, I want to work with my sister Ephah, and—"

"Of course," said Ester. "Help Gath and the others with the ladders."

The Samaritan woman presented herself to Joseph. "I'm Abatal."

"All right." Joseph shook his head with astonishment. "Join us, Abatal."

He and Abatal, Ephah and Tamar, and several other women plodded to where numerous ladders were stacked, and where Gath awaited them.

Nicodemus glanced at Ester. "We can release his ankles while they get the ladders."

"Then let's do it."

They approached the foot of the cross. She caressed Jesus' left foot with both her hands.

"There's no time for that."

"Tenderness will accompany the care he receives from us," Ester countered, firmly.

Nicodemus was not used to a woman rebuking him in public. He pressed his lips together. "Right." He peered at the nearby guards. "Let's get started. I fear these Romans are beginning to lose their patience."

Ester stole a glance at the guards. "They have no patience. Believe me. I've been here all day. They're simply bored. They'll leave you alone."

"Why?"

"Because you're among women now and, therefore, you're unimportant." Ester noted Nicodemus' repulsion of the idea. Her chuckle deepened his resentment. "Get over it. It's not so bad becoming invisible."

CHAPTER 11

Mother

The rain stopped. The sky intensified. The wind veered. The carrion birds disappeared.

Ester tore her eyes away from her Master's broken feet and searched the sky. "What does this mean?"

Several women crept up from behind and huddled near the heavy wooden stake that held their Lord's body.

"That his death is final," said Nicodemus.

Ester touched Jesus' torn and bloody feet. "But our Jesus said it wasn't. Didn't you listen to him?"

"Then look," said Nicodemus. "And touch. Do you believe in everything you hear?"

Ester kissed Jesus' right foot. "I believe in him. That's all I know. That's all I know."

The odd darkness and the sky's strangeness and the sudden stillness unnerved everybody.

A harsh voice intruded. "Get on with it!"

Nicodemus dropped his hammer and chisel. Ester released her Master's feet. The other women stirred from their trances.

Strabo approached them. "Seal or no seal, if I lose my patience—"

Nicodemus clapped his hands at the women as he acknowledged the guard. "All right. All right! Let's get to it as the guard commands us."

Strabo laughed. He nodded sinisterly at Nicodemus, then turned away from him and sauntered back to his post.

Nicodemus picked up his hammer and chisel, then waved the tools at the surrounding women like a baton. "Stand back for those who are bringing the ladders. Go on. Stand back. You. Help with the ladders. And you. Clear away that jar."

The women accelerated their activity. One of them took away the bowl of posca and sponge. Another set an enclosed oil lamp nearby. And several left the foot of the cross to see if they could assist in transporting ladders.

Nicodemus approached Jesus' battered and blackened feet. He wedged the chisel between Jesus' left ankle and the wood, after Ester pulled the ankle as far from the stake as the spike's head would allow.

"Watch yourself," said Nicodemus. "I'm not very good with a hammer and chisel."

"Then you'll have to do the best you can."

"Hmm. You women have grown fearless."

"Grown? We die in childbirth every day, and only now we've grown fearless?"

"Hmm. Forgive my . . . my blindness." Nicodemus struck the head of the chisel.

"Do you mean that?"

He carefully aimed the hammer. "Mean what?"

"I heard the strained tone in your voice."

"Strained. Perhaps. But did you listen to my words? Look out." He struck the head of the chisel.

"Women always have to listen for the true meaning of what is said to them." She released her left hand from Jesus' foot to allow Nicodemus the freedom to swing the hammer harder and with greater confidence. "Then, these next few hours together must stand by themselves, I fear."

"I'm sorry."

Ester looked up at Jesus. "He will prevail, somehow. Somehow. He was always kind to women and children. Always. We were not invisible to him." She prompted Nicodemus. "Strike harder."

Nicodemus put greater strength behind the third blow. Jesus' left ankle came free of the wood. "There."

Ester lowered Jesus' left foot, allowing the weight of the limb to extend the leg. She pulled the severed spike from his ankle by its head. Blood oozed onto her right hand. "Dear God." She dropped the bloody spike inside the void above her belted tunic. "The other."

They positioned themselves on Jesus' right side.

"You can hand me the hammer and chisel if you like," Ester offered.

"Don't be silly."

"You look like you're going to get sick."

"The sight of blood and torn skin. Yes. I feel a little sick to my—"

"Here. Let me—"

"No."

Ester frowned. "Women are use to blood and torn skin. Midwives and mothers and—"

"Yes, yes, yes. And Jesus had difficulties with scholars like me."

"Yes. With all aristocrats of the priestly establishment." Ester took hold of Jesus' right foot and maneuvered her body so Nicodemus could wedge the chisel between the ankle and the wood again. "Which you are part of."

"I'm a Pharisee. Not a priest." He struck the chisel with the hammer. "I'll not apologize for who I am."

"I'm not asking you to."

"I see. Like our Master, you want to identify things and people as they are." Nicodemus aimed the hammer.

"I suppose. Yes." Ester raised her head in anticipation of Nicodemus' unsteady blow and saw her Master's injured penis lying across the right side of the wooden support peg, which had been sculpted into a grotesquely large circumcised penis in order to further humiliate the King of Jews. His male appendage was deeply black and blue from the repeated blows it had received. Ester understood what pain from the center of one's being was about: the violation of rape, and the twelve-year constancy of menstruation had caused her tremendous suffering and humiliation. Her Master must have tasted something of this central pain and suffering that was common among women. "Hit the spike hard."

Nicodemus struck and sheared the spike on the second blow. "Good." His face showed satisfaction. "I . . . I secretly admit that women often have a better ability to see things as they are."

Ester lowered Jesus' leg, removed the bloody spike from his right ankle, and dropped it inside her tunic with the other. "That's high recognition coming from . . . from someone like you. But then, you and your approaching colleague there have demonstrated that you are not like the rest."

"There are others," Nicodemus asserted.

"If you say so."

"There are. Believe me."

"They should have done something as well."

"There wasn't enough time. No way to figure out a solution."

"I see." Ester kissed Jesus' torn right foot. "I loved him."

"So did I."

"Where do you want these four ladders?" Joseph inquired. Behind him stood Gath and Tamar on the opposite ends of a ladder, as well as Abatal and Ephah, Joseph and Mara, and two others—all, were paired at the opposite ends of their respective ladders.

Several more women swelled their ranks at the foot of Jesus' cross. Among them were: Mara, the wife of Peter; Shelomith, the mother-in-law of Peter;

Hanna, the pregnant wife of Aaron; Mary, the wife of Clopas; Salome, the mother of James and John; Joanna, the wife of Chuza; Susanna, the wealthiest of their patronesses; and Blessed Mother, who took no part in handling the ladders but who stood by with Blessed Sister and Mary of Magdala, and waited for her son to be lowered into her arms.

"Two ladders on either side of the right and left crossbeams," Nicodemus directed. "Be careful, this is still a terrible day despite the cessation of rain. The lightning. Be careful. The lightning."

A very old woman, unknown to them all, and much too frail to assist in any other way than to provide the solidarity of her presence, stared at the limp-legged figure straddled on the grotesque wooden peg. Jesus' legs dangled from the impact of the four raised ladders slamming against both sides of the crossbeam. The old woman raised her thin arms upward to him and chanted: "*'Eloi, Eloi, lema sabachthani?'* That's what he said." She lowered her weak arms. She sought somebody's attention. Any woman. Any woman's eye. "What . . . what does that mean if God forsook him? Him. What does that mean to us? To all of us. To any of us."

Hanna placed a sympathetic hand on the elderly woman's shoulder. "Calm yourself, grandmother."

"But I don't understand, my child."

"Everything will be revealed in its own time."

"Tamar, hold this ladder still," Gath directed, as she climbed the ladder that leaned on the front right crossbeam.

Hanna affectionately squeezed the old woman's shoulder. Together, they watched the others tend to the ladders.

"It's a shame we can't take down the other two," Tamar muttered.

"There's nothing we can do for them," Joseph announced emphatically. "Nothing. Don't—" He caught sight of Dinah, who was sitting on the ground before Azriel's cross. He whispered. "Don't stir that woman. She's possessed by demons."

"She's a woman who mourns for her man." Ester stood at the foot of the ladder that leaned against the rear left crossbeam, which also supported Nicodemus.

"Not unlike us." Abatal stood midway up the ladder that leaned against the front left crossbeam. Like the other women, who had climbed midway up the ladders, she was positioned to help lower Jesus to his awaiting mother, and aunt, and . . .

"Don't compare that man with our Master," Joseph barked.

"She was talking about that woman and us," said Ephah, from the foot of the ladder that supported Abatal. "You idiot." She turned away from Joseph and addressed Abatal. "Men."

Abatal acknowledged her sister from above. "It's always about men."

Joseph felt surrounded and outnumbered, unpopular and outranked, despite his position and his present intent. He sought Nicodemus, who was already perched on top of the ladder that leaned against the rear left crossbeam. He was positioned over his Master's left arm with a hammer in one hand and a chisel in the other.

Nicodemus shrugged his shoulders to indicate that he was unable to help him. "Climb the other ladder, my friend."

Joseph shrugged his shoulders to display his helplessness and to convey a half apology to the women. He suddenly realized that everybody was waiting for him. "Sorry."

The numerous ladders that were propped against his Master's cross looked like a vertical latticework of scaffolding. Mara and another woman, who were patiently waiting for Joseph to climb the unoccupied ladder that leaned against the rear right crossbeam, frowned at him.

"Sorry," Joseph repeated, as he approached the foot of the ladder and gingerly climbed to the top. He neither liked the height nor the unsteadiness of the ladder. He held onto the crossbeam while Mara climbed up midway to help lower Jesus to the women below; the movement of the ladder as she climbed into position frightened him.

After Nicodemus was confident that everybody was securely in place, he sought Blessed Mother, Blessed Sister, and Mary of Magdala, who were waiting patiently below. "Are you ready to receive him?"

"We are ready," said Mary.

Nicodemus leaned hard against the ladder, then reached precariously over the crossbeam with the hammer and chisel in order to release Jesus' left wrist from the wood. He wedged the chisel between the back of Jesus' wrist and the front of the beam, raised the hammer seriously high into the sky, and with one blow sheared the spike from the wood and released his Master's wrist from the instrument of his torture.

The women, who stood midway up the ladder, almost lost their footing by the sudden shift in the body; they held Jesus in place.

"Well done," said Ester.

Nicodemus glanced at Joseph, then looked down at Ester. "Thank you."

"Keep him steady up there," Tamar whispered to Gath.

"I'll not let him fall," said the old slave woman. "Don't worry."

Nicodemus leaned toward Joseph, who reached for the chisel and hammer. Joseph's left foot slipped off the rung of the ladder, but he held on to the right crossbeam.

"Careful, my friend," said Nicodemus.

"I'm getting old." Joseph got hold of the tools, then straightened himself out on the ladder. He studied the hammer and chisel. "May God guide my unsteady hands."

"You'll be all right. Hurry." Nicodemus reached over the crossbeam and assisted Ester with the weight of Jesus. She had climbed midway up the ladder without waiting for another woman to take her place at the foot of the ladder. "Hurry."

When Joseph reached over the crossbeam, he

almost lost his footing again. He dropped the chisel and almost hit one of the women below.

"Hey! Look out up there," Ephah squawked.

"Sorry."

"You almost killed Tamar."

"I'm all right."

"I'm not young anymore," Joseph muttered.

"Then you should have allowed one of us to—"

"I can do this. Send up the chisel."

Tamar picked up the chisel, still shaken by the near miss, and gave it to the woman, who stood at the foot of the nearby ladder. She passed the chisel up to Mara, who stood midway up the ladder below Joseph.

"Are you sure I can't take your place?" Mara whispered, to avoid embarrassing the old man.

"Never. Give me the chisel."

"Right." Mara offered the chisel to him. "May God listen to you this time."

Joseph pressed his lips together in order to prevent himself from losing his temper. He snatched the chisel from her hand. "Thank you."

Mara grinned. "You're welcome."

Joseph ignored her malice and tried to concentrate. His hands trembled. Everyone waited for him to release the Messiah from the instrument of his torture and death.

He wedged the chisel between the back of Jesus' wrist and the wooden crossbeam, tapped the head of the spike with the hammer in order to orient his aim, then raised the hammer. "Lord." He closed his eyes and swung the hammer down upon the head of the spike with all of his might.

The sound of the hammer hitting the chisel's head, the sound of the hammer's handle hitting the crossbeam, and the sound of the chisel's cutting edge shearing the spike in two was simultaneous.

Miraculously, Joseph did not hurt his hand, and the dropped hammer did not hit anybody below. Nobody complained this time.

Jesus slumped forward on the support peg between his legs. The women carefully lifted Jesus to maneuver his right leg over the support peg and lower his broken body into his mother's arms. The women on the ground assisted to ensure Blessed Mother's safety, as well as to prevent any further damage to the body.

Pianissimo cries rose to the heavens from the earthbound women in mourning. A strange harmony developed from the voices of too many kinds of sorrow.

As soon as Jesus was nestled in his mother's arms, Mary of Magdala unfolded a clean white linen sheet and covered the lower portion of Jesus' naked body. The blood from his wounds, particularly from his groin, soaked through the inside of the linen to the outer surface in thick red blotches.

A steady rain began to fall again, which soaked the blood stained sheet and spread the scarlet hue from the groin to the hips and thighs. Rape and violation could not be concealed with linen.

Everybody grew still and silent after Mary of

Magdala knelt beside the Mother of Jesus to give her support and comfort. Those left on the ladders bowed their heads, those on the ground dropped to their knees.

Someone had laid their cloak on the ground for Blessed Mother to sit on, as well as to keep the lower portion of her son's body from sinking into the mud.

Blessed Mother lifted the crown of thorns from her son's bloody head with her left hand and flung the despicable object into the outer darkness with the power of a mother's strength. Then she rocked her son: his head against her breasts, her right arm supporting his back, and her left arm embracing his chest. All the tenderness in the world could be seen in this mother's affection. Only the wind and the rain and the thunder dared to intrude.

Eternity passed before Blessed Mother could find the strength to speak. Her whisper was heard by everyone who wanted to listen:

"Child's mind, beginner's mind. That's what I would say of him if asked to describe him in a few words. He was not like other children and, yet, he played and sang and was difficult to discipline because he was generous beyond our means: giving support to the weaker, food to the poorer, and encouragement to the defeated. I still see the joy he caused and hear the laughter of a child's mind. I still see the warmth in his heart and feel the constancy of his unpretentious beginner's mind. I still see his suffering and tremble with sorrowful tears at the foot of his cross."

The women who were perched on the ladders and the men who were stooped over the crossbeams for support, descended to the ground so slowly that it appeared as if portions of the cross were melting with the rain. Each of them dropped to their knees as soon as their feet touched the hallowed ground.

Blessed Mother caressed Jesus more intensely, then kissed him. "My son, my first born. My dear Immanuel."

"What did Blessed Mother call him?" a woman whispered to her companion.

"Immanuel," the companion whispered, more cautiously than the questioner.

"I thought he was called Joshua," she muttered, close to her companion's ear.

The companion cupped her right hand over her mouth. "By the angel, yes."

The questioner was perplexed. "All right."

The companion clarified her remark. "He was called Joshua by the angel, Immanuel by the prophet, and Messiah by the scribes."

"Ohhh!" The questioner placed both hands over her mouth after responding too loudly. "So, that's how the story goes?"

"That's part of it."

"No wonder the Romans were confused and gave him the title King."

"They were not confused. Greeks. Romans. Hebrews."

"Where?"

"Up there. Written on the placard above his head."

"Oh."

"The letters are the same in Aramaic."

"You can read?"

"Of course not." She pointed to another woman. "She read me the inscription that identifies his so-called crime to Rome: *'This is Jesus, the King of the Judeans.'*"

"But he was a Galilean."

"Shhh. Look. Speaking of Rome. The guards are approaching."

"All right, all right. This is all very touching." Strabo scowled at Joseph. "You. The one with Pilate's seal. You may have orders from Pilate permitting you to take this man's body, but those orders don't include this public indulgence. Away with you all. I've grown bored with the lot of you." He stomped on the ground and purposely splashed mud onto Blessed Mother.

The surrounding women stirred with resentment.

Joseph raised his hand as if he were going to protest. He checked himself.

"What." Strabo took a threatening step toward Joseph. "Go ahead. Say something."

Nicodemus nudged Joseph to be silent.

"That's right," said Strabo. "You'd better not say anything if you want to see another day, old man."

"Careful," Vespa whispered. "Remember their influence."

"Possible influence, you idiot."

"Whatever. Remember, there's worse duty than this. I don't want to share that with you."

"Bah."

"I learned this from you, remember? I'm the one without the brains."

Strabo was surprised by Vespa's moment of clarity. "Now I understand why I bother to keep you at my side." Strabo turned to Joseph and Nicodemus. "I said away with you all, if you're going to take this body. Otherwise, it stays, orders or no orders."

Several women hurried to Blessed Mother's side and lifted Jesus from her. Mary of Magdala and Blessed Sister assisted Blessed Mother to her feet.

"Come on, dear. Come with us."

"Yes," said Joseph. "There's a dwelling nearby that we can take him to, in order to prepare his body."

"Whose place?" Ester inquired, standing as the leader of the women in attendance.

"A secret disciple with wealth and standing," said Nicodemus. "My place."

"Our Master could have used your help long before now." Ester could not control her rekindled resentment.

"I know, I know," said Nicodemus. "But you must remember: our Master took the help he wanted. Not what was offered."

"No, no," said Ester. "That's a very nice justification."

"Yes, yes," said Joseph, in Nicodemus' defense. "It was written. Didn't you listen to him? He said so, many times. Many times."

"I didn't see you many times with him," Ester insisted, trying to control her increasing resentment.

Strabo interrupted them all, once again. "I told you people to get out!"

"You'd better hurry," said Vespa. "He's a crazy man. I won't be able to stop him once he truly loses his temper."

A ragged formation quickly assembled.

Nicodemus led the procession toward their intended destination. Joseph protected the procession's rear.

CHAPTER 12

Procession

The wind veered, then intensified as the procession moved toward its destination. The severity of this natural force alarmed all who were following Jesus' body to the place where he was going to be bathed and anointed before burial; the wind's debris assaulted every eye, every mind laid waste by what they thought to be the elemental breath of God.

Darkness.

The persistent daytime gloom plagued their shadowed spirits and made them clutch more tightly to their outer garments.

Cold.

The bitterness penetrated the backs of their

minds, forcing them to hunch forward and intensify the composition of their grief.

Weary.

The lightning and thunder violated the senses of their souls, eliminating their memories and obscuring their hope for a future.

Sorrowful.

The rain drenched the course wool of their ragged beings, increasing their weight and slowing down their progress.

Who was this man they were holding in their arms? What was going to happen without their Messiah? Where was that powerful dynamic called faith?

Alone. Each of them felt dark. Cold. Weary. Sorrowful. Alone.

One of the sisters who supported Jesus' shoulders stumbled when she stepped into a mud hole that the procession's guide, Nicodemus, had not seen. The procession shuddered from the misstep, from the momentary halt in progress, and from the clumsy recovery. By the time Joseph of Arimathea, the caretaker of the procession's rear, inquired about the sudden delay, the procession began to advance again.

The bleak landscape did not provide any visual comfort. Death seemed to have consumed the meaning of Jesus' existence, which left these mourners blind and barren.

When they reached a courtyard's entrance attached to a large dwelling, Nicodemus struck the solid wooden gate with the back of his right fist.

The walls of the structure were made of stone without mortar, and the roof of the dwelling was made of sticks and reeds, which were thickly coated with clay that had hardened from the baking sun and, therefore, had made the roof resistant to the rain.

The gate swung open as if the person behind it had been expecting visitors. A servant woman appeared with a stoic expression. She bowed to Nicodemus, peered at the stalled procession behind him, then stepped aside for Nicodemus to enter the dwelling's complex.

The procession passed through the gate and entered the courtyard, where several women were hastily completing the cooking and the baking before the light of the uncertain gray sky was lost and became the certain darkness that ushered in this Passover's Sabbath.

Nicodemus directed the women carrying Jesus' body to the left, and through a door leading into a large interior chamber with a table prepared to receive the body. Then he personally escorted Blessed Mother, Blessed Sister, and Mary of Magdala into another room so they could wait in comfort, as well as receive those who were close to them. The others in the procession filled the courtyard and offered assistance to the household's servants.

Tamar, who carried Jesus by his right shoulder, bumped Jesus' head against the doorjamb.

"Careful." said Ephah, who carried Jesus by his left hip.

"Sorry."

"That's no way to treat our Rabbi." Mara had Jesus' calves resting on her shoulders.

"I loved him too!" Tamar snapped.

"Quiet." Ester held Jesus by his left shoulder. "And calm yourselves. Let's get him inside."

"Ester's right." Abatal supported Jesus' right hip.

With extra caution, they maneuvered Jesus through the door into a well-lighted room and laid him on the table. Salome, Hanna, and Gath, who followed them inside, dispersed into the room to see what had been provided for the cleansing and anointing of his body.

Oil lamps flickered in all four corners of the room.

Gath peered through one of two small windows set high on the wall. "You'd think it was midnight from the darkness of the sky."

"I'm frightened," said Ephah. "Will we ever see the light again?"

"What does it matter?" said Ester.

Lightning flashed intensely, brightening the windows like eyes into the night.

"Bring two of those oil lamps to the table, Hanna," said Mara.

Nicodemus entered the room. "I'll leave you ladies to attend to his preparation." He pointed his finger. "In that jar, underneath the table, there are several pounds of myrrh and—"

"I've already found it," said Abatal.

"Good. Good."

"There are washcloths and bowls and filled water jars in the next room and—"

"Leave it to us," said Salome. "I'm sure everything we need is here."

"Everything," Nicodemus emphasized.

"We'll call for you if we need anything."

"Anything. Anything. Let me or Joseph know."

"We will."

Nicodemus stopped at the entranceway on his way out of the room. "I have food prepared for those of you—"

"I'm not hungry," Ester said.

"Neither am I," said Tamar.

Despite their all-day fast on the streets of Jerusalem and on the grounds of Golgotha, none of them were hungry.

"Yes. Well. There is food and drink available." Nicodemus pointed at another door. "There are additional water jars and washbowls in there." He wrung his hands together. "Linen sheets and wraps are on a shelf. More aloe and myrrh are in several thick jars. There's plenty, plenty more. And there's another door in there leading outside to discard unclean water."

"You mean, his blood," Ester said, with growing impatience.

"Yes. His blood. Yes. Into the ground. There's . . . there's no other place for it." He scanned the room. "Please, hurry. I'll be back shortly to check on your progress. Remember, there's not much time left." He stepped across the doorway's threshold. "The tomb is freshly cut and awaiting him."

"Who's providing it?" asked Salome.

"Joseph."

"God bless you both," said Hanna.

"Nothing. We've done nothing." Nicodemus peered at Jesus' body. "He looks so . . . so ordinary in here and . . . and, on that table."

"Death reduces all of us to that," said Gath.

"Right. Right." Nicodemus shut the door behind himself.

"Nervous as a cat," Gath remarked. "Men. Squeamish, squeamish men."

Several women sneered.

"Where's your mother and mother-in-law?" Hanna asked Mara, in order to change the subject.

"With Blessed Mother," said Mara.

"Good."

"I saw to that myself," Salome interjected.

"Thank you," said Mara.

"Susanna and Joanna and Martha are attending to her, as well."

Hanna's smile of approval was the first of its kind today among these women. "Then Blessed Mother is in good hands."

"Thank, God," said Mara.

Ester pulled the blood soaked sheet off of Jesus' broken body. Most of them gasped.

"My God," said Ephah. "His injuries appear more horrible in here."

"We certainly have our work cut out for us." Ester glanced at Mara and Salome. "Go see what we have in the next room." She peered at Hanna. "Stay with him. He should not be left without prayer."

"I will." Hanna placed her right hand on Jesus'

upper arm. "I'm here." She touched the underside of her seven-month belly with her left hand, then turned to Gath. "But I must relieve myself first. Please—"

"Of course, my dear. I'll not leave his side until you return."

Salome and Mara migrated into the other room to assess what was actually in there.

Ester pulled out the bowls, the washcloths, and the myrrh from underneath the table. "Tamar, bring in more washbowls. Ephah and Abatal, carry in more water. Gath, bring in more washcloths as soon as Hanna returns." She called into the other chamber. "Mara, more spices."

Mara entered the room carrying a large jar in her arms. "Look. The spices have already been mixed."

"And look," said Salome, as she entered the room, "These linen wraps are already impregnated."

"Good," said Ester. "Good. All this will save us time." She clapped her hands. "Let's go, ladies. There's not much time left before nightfall."

The women responded with the calm experience of mothers and midwives and nurses. The care of bodies—the sick and the young, the fragile and the broken, the living and the dead—was a common duty among women. Blood and dirt, as well as the familiar odor of vomit and feces, were common components of their domestic chores.

They approached Jesus with water and washcloths, as well as with love and tenderness. The sound of washcloths being rinsed and wrung out filled the room.

Ester wiped a black crust of blood from Jesus' fore-head with her wet washcloth. She turned her cloth over and studied the filth. "Lord. We're going to need a lot of water."

"Don't worry," said Ephah. "Abatal and I will take care of that."

The activity of scrubbing Jesus' body filled the chamber.

Hanna entered the room and approached Gath, who was glad to be released from the duty of prayers. Now Gath was free to find more washcloths, and help scrub her Master's body clean. Hanna placed a small jar near Jesus' feet before occupying Gath's place at Jesus' side.

"What's that?" Ester asked.

"Spikenard oil to cleanse his feet."

"These men have provided us with all that we need."

"I just promised Mary, Lazuras' sister, that I would cleanse his feet from what was left in her heartfelt jar of lotion that she wished to contribute. I promised her."

"Of course, yes, of course. I suppose she's with Blessed Mother."

"Yes. She and her sister Martha are attending to her."

"Understood. May I assist you?"

"Please," said Hanna. "Honor me."

Ester dipped her hand into the jar and applied some of the lotion to his right foot, and Hanna did the same to his left foot. The lotion loosened some of the dirt and the dried blood from his feet. Satisfied that she had fulfilled her promise to Mary, Hanna returned to Jesus' side to pray while Ester wiped off the brown and bloody paste from his feet with a clean wash-cloth.

CHAPTER 13

Anointed

The two flickering oil lamps, which Hanna had placed near Jesus' body, accentuated the stillness of his remains.

Hanna's large and dark brown eyes shined brightly from her youthful face, from her marble clear complexion, and from her delicate features; her sincerity of prayer filled the room as the others bathed Jesus' body. Mara's stern face, in direct contrast, was the product of a difficult marriage with Peter; she carefully placed a large washbowl by Hanna's feet.

Gath returned to Hanna's side with fresh washcloths. She set them on the table, near Jesus' left side, rinsed one of the cloths in the bowl Mara had provided, and scrubbed Jesus' chest. When she finally had to rinse the washcloth in the bowl, she caught Mara's attention. Gath whispered. "I saw him."

"Who?"

"Your husband. I thought you'd like to know."

Mara bit her lower lip. "Yes. Where?"

"I saw him sitting in the outer gloom of the fire that I was tending in the middle of the courtyard near the hall where the Sanhedrin had called their meeting." Both women pretended to clean their Master as Gath shared what she knew about Mara's husband as discreetly as possible. The other women pretended not to listen. "He avoided my eyes, but I recognized him all right—and he knew it. 'You're one of them,' I said. 'Leave me alone,' he answered. Then he asked, 'Who are you?' I was surprised."

"How come?"

"Well, I'm a slave. An old woman. A nothing. Nobody asks me that. Nobody. 'Well,' I said, 'I'm as you see, a slave tending a fire.' I was prepared to let it go, when my sister in labor inquired what I was talking about, as she entered the courtyard with a sack full of charcoal. 'What's this about a nobody?' my old sister asked, as she added more charcoal to the fire. So I said to her, 'I said, this fellow was with him, too. You know, with the one that's on trial in there.' My charcoal-bearing sister peered over the fire as I poked the coals with my iron. 'Ahh, Jesus.' Then she squinted at Peter. 'You know that man?' Well, you should have seen him turn gray. 'My good woman,' he said. 'I don't know him.'" Gath clapped her hands.

"Just like that. He denied him outright. With no shame. Then he said, 'Don't look at me that way, it's the truth.' My sister in labor countered, 'He sounds like a Galilean to me.' And that was enough for him to move away from us." Gath noted the anger in Mara's eyes. "I'm sorry."

"That's all right." Mara clenched her teeth. She dropped her washcloth into the washbowl. "I wanted to know. We need a fresh washbowl."

Gath nodded. "Sure. Sure."

The others remained silent and ignored Mara's personal tragedy. They bathed his body, and oiled his wounds.

Mara walked unsteadily toward the door leading into the other chamber. They heard her weeping before she entered the room.

Ester caressed the top of Jesus' damaged scrotum with a clean washcloth, then gently wiped off some of the blood and dirt, urine and feces.

The limp washcloth, smeared with his bodily fluids, drooped from her right hand that hovered above his genitals. She studied what was left of Jesus:

Large chunks of his scalp were missing. There were deep puncture wounds on his forehead, on his temples, and on the back of his head. Because the crown of thorns had been pounded onto his head, many of the puncture wounds were also torn. His left eye had been gouged out of its socket; his right eye was black and swollen. The left nostril of his broken nose was ripped and his lips were cracked. His right earlobe was missing, and his left earlobe was split in half. His face was crisscrossed with cuts and scratches as if his features had been covered by an abstract image painted on a muslin cloth so thin and loosely woven and transparent that the material allowed the abstraction to appear etched across his ruined face.

His neck was rope burned, and the front and back of his torso was shredded. His arms, as well as his hands and feet, were bloody and torn: there wasn't a single fingernail left on any digit; all fingers and toes were either black, or a sickly shade of blue.

Exposed bone. Torn flesh. Missing hair. Broken teeth.

Ester reached underneath his scrotum and verified that he was missing his left testicle; she understood the pain he must have suffered in this tender, most private area of a person's body. The center of her Master's being had been violated.

Like the rest of him, Jesus' flaccid penis was bruised and lacerated, torn and reduced to the raw nakedness of death. The result of this mistreatment was the only evidence that falsely characterized him as a criminal.

Tears flowed from Ester's eyes. "I swear to God, I wish you were not dead. In your name, I swear to God—"

"Ester, please." Salome's tone was careful. Gentle. Respectful. "You should not swear to the Lord."

"Our Jesus did. Many, many times."

"He always did things we did not understand and . . . and look. Where did it get him?"

Ester studied the red, black, and brown smears on her washcloth. "Where have you gone, my Lord? Where has he gone, Salome?"

"To his end."

Ester placed the palm of her left hand on Jesus' thigh. "Take me with you."

"Control yourself."

"Take me with you." Ester rinsed the soiled washcloth in the large bowl of water. The clear water turned into a reddish-brown solution. She lifted the cloth out of the bowl and wrung out the excess water. She stared at his damaged scrotum and his lacerated penis. She was saddened by the severity of his torture. She brushed the washcloth across his genitals, maneuvered it between his legs, then slipped the cloth underneath his scrotum. She scooped out a crusty blood clot embedded in his hardened feces. "I have not abandoned you, my Lord." She shook the foul particles from the washcloth and dropped the cloth into the bowl. "See? I have remained with you even beyond your death on the cross. See? We refuse to scatter. And yet, I and what I have been able to perceive of the others here, do not possess your peace. Where is the peace? What is this peace you spoke about?"

Salome placed her right hand on Ester's shoulder, as Abatal exchanged Ester's blood-filled washbowl with another bowl of water. "It is getting late, Ester."

"Sorry." Ester reached into the fresh bowl of water, wrung out the washcloth, and continued to clean his genitals.

"He is beyond our inquiry." Salome removed her hand from Ester's shoulder. "I'm sorry."

"Yes. Yes."

"The Sabbath is approaching," Tamar added. "Hurry." She had finished cleaning his face and upper body. "I don't mean to interfere with your—"

"Sorrow. I know that."

"We all have our secrets with him," said Abatal. "Private and public."

"I know, I know." Ester's restiveness intensified.

"I'm sorry," said Abatal. "I didn't mean to interfere—"

"But the time, the time, I know. You're right." Ester wrung out her washcloth and wiped off his inner right thigh. "Keep me steady, Salome. Abatal. All of you. Help me continue to serve him."

"We're all doing that for each other," said Hanna.

Ester swallowed hard, but she failed to hold back her tears. She refused to sniffle, despite the congestion in her nose.

"Are you going to be all right?" Ephah whispered.

"Yes, yes, of course." Ester concentrated on her work.

Ephah gazed at Jesus' head. "Look at those bruises and cuts and, oh, what that crown of thorns did to him. Poor, poor baby." She stroked Jesus' battered head.

"What's happening to us?" Salome sought everybody's attention. "We've prepared bodies before."

Ephah stopped stroking his head. "I shouldn't have spoken."

"I'm sorry. I didn't mean to embarrass anybody."

"I feel small and . . ." Ephah dropped her arms to her side, ". . . and you were truly with him."

"He was with us all," Salome admonished. "We are with him now. Equally. Equally."

"Salome's right," Ester muttered. "He was with us all."

"Yes," Abatal added. "And we all feel small, Ephah."

They continued bathing his body.

"His hair needs washing and combing," said Tamar.

Gath pursed her lips. "There's no time for that."

"I'll wash his hair," Mara declared. She entered the main room brandishing a comb. "And I'll comb his hair."

They intensified their efforts. Abatal provided fresh water. Gath replaced washcloths. Salome brought more jars of the prepared aloe and myrrh mixtures to the table. Ester and Tamar and Ephah scrubbed and wiped. Hanna prayed.

"Let's slide him toward the head of the table." Mara hooked her left hand under Jesus' right armpit, and waited for Tamar to hook her right hand under his left armpit. Together they pulled Jesus toward the head of the table with Ephah guiding his head over the edge. Abatal set a large pitcher of fresh water on the floor near the head of the table, then filled a large washbowl with water.

"Bring that over here," said Mara.

Abatal maneuvered the bowl underneath Jesus'

head and raised it up to immerse his dangling hair. She held the bowl in place while Ephah steadied his head by supporting his neck.

Mara washed his hair. The grime and blood softened in the water. Mara used her fingers to untangle the large knots, and break up the numerous clots that held his hair in bunches.

"Do you need any help?" Ephah asked.

"Just hold him steady."

"The water needs changing already," said Abatal.

"Here's a fresh bowl." Tamar exchanged her clean bowl for Abatal's dirty one. "Do you need any help holding up that bowl?"

"No," said Abatal.

"But that bowl of water is so heavy."

"She's stronger than any three of us put together," said Ephah.

"I have it," Abatal insisted.

"All right," said Tamar.

They washed his hair, and finished scrubbing his neck, arms, and torso; his genitals, legs, and feet. Then they slid Jesus down the table, turned him onto his side, and washed the back of everything.

Ester cleaned his filthy, torn buttocks. His anal crevice was caked with blood and feces and dark sand. "Oh, my God."

"Easy, dear."

The stench of urine and sweat and fecal matter engulfed them. Despite being use to childbearing and child rearing, with all the familiar smells of vomit and perspiration, and despite being use to cradle deaths and miscarriages, these veteran caretakers of the dead were still overwhelmed by the harsh odors that arose from their Master's violated body.

"We are running out of time," said Ester.

"His hair is washed and combed," said Mara.

"And his body is cleansed," Ephah added.

Ester acknowledged their reports with a nod. "Then let's anoint him."

They dipped their right hands into the jars of aloe and myrrh, and lovingly spread the oily mixture onto their Master's body.

Ester took charge of caring for their Master's privacy. She spread the aloe and myrrh mixture onto Jesus' damaged genitals and inserted the oiled tips of her fingers into the raw crevice leading to his rectum. She was startled when a surge of energy suddenly coursed through her body.

"What."

Ester turned away from Salome, as she eased her fingers away. "Nothing." Her right hand trembled. "Nothing."

"Are you all right?" Salome asked.

"I . . . I don't know. A strange feeling flowed through my body and my limbs like a cold stream of water. I . . . I've never felt so strange. I . . ." Ester placed her right hand into the nearest jar of the aloe and myrrh mixture. The coolness of the oil calmed her. She scooped out some of the mixture and massaged the back of his right thigh.

The other women averted their eyes from what Ester was doing as they anointed his body.

"Very well." Mara stood back from Jesus. "I believe we are ready to apply those spiced linen wraps."

The sudden change in activity broke Ester's trance. She looked at Salome.

"Are you all right?" Salome whispered.

"No."

Gath gave two thick rolls of linen wrap, impregnated with oil and spices, to Salome. "Wrap his legs." She gave rolls to Tamar and Abatal. "His arms." She gave a single roll to Mara. "His head." She peered at Ephah. "Help me with his torso. You too, Hanna." She avoided Ester. She realized Ester was temporarily possessed. She also realized that her sister disciples would never talk about this possession.

They bound Jesus' arms and hands, his legs and feet by unrolling the linen wraps around his limbs. They covered his body with great love and care, with tender silence and attention.

Ester slipped a wide linen cloth underneath Jesus' buttocks after Salome and Abatal lifted his hips from the table. "Good." The women lowered Jesus' hips. Then Ester brought the lower portion of the wide cloth up to his abdomen from between his legs and overlapped the two ends, on both sides of his waist, like a diaper. The sticky wetness of the spiced linen cloth acted like glue and kept the diaper in place. Ester stepped back from the foot of the table. "Should we unroll a linen wrap around his waist?"

"No," said Salome. "That should hold."

With the binding process complete, Mara disappeared into the other room, then reappeared with a very large folded linen sheet: white and long and tight in weave. Gath, Tamar, and Hanna helped Mara unwrap the large shroud while Ester and Salome, Abatal and Ephah rolled Jesus toward the edge of the table onto his side. After the lower half of the shroud was spread along the full length of the table, Jesus was rolled onto his back. Then just as Gath and Tamar were about to fold the upper half of the shroud over the top of Jesus, Ester shouted, "Wait!" Ester snatched a clean linen cloth from Mara's hand.

"What are you doing?" Mara demanded. "What's wrong?"

"This is it," Ester said calmly. "This will be—" She peered at the other women. "This will be the last time I—we—shall ever see his face again."

"Have faith," said Salome. "Remember?"

"Easy for you to say." The tone in Ester's voice flattened. "He said many things. But . . . but look at him. He's—"

"Stop thinking," said Mara, "and cover his face. The Passover's Sabbath is approaching."

"Mara is right," said Tamar.

"He's depending on us," Hanna added.

"Us. Yes. Us." Ester smiled. "We who are invisible. We who will be forgotten."

"That doesn't matter," said Salome. "Remember. Nothing matters. Nothing but the love of God and the love of each other."

Ester nodded. "He said that, I remember."

Abatal placed a gentle hand on Ester's shoulder. "Finish it. Please."

Ester unfolded the clean linen cloth. "Look at him. How beautiful. I'm glad his mouth is closed." She laid the cloth over his face. "There. It is finished."

Then Gath and Tamar folded the top half of the shroud over the full length of Jesus' body.

Hanna suddenly called attention to her prayers by violently ripping a small tear in her tunic. "Blessed are you, the true judge."

Ester tore her tunic as well. "Blessed are you, the true judge."

The sound of tearing followed among the others:

"Blessed are you, the—"

"True judge."

"Blessed—"

". . . the true—"

". . . are you, the true—"

"Blessed are—"

"Ladies, ladies, please. Is our Master's body prepared?" Joseph inquired. The women were startled by his intrusion. "I'm sorry. I did not want to interrupt your prayers but—"

"What must be done now?" Salome inquired.

"I have provided a bier to have him transported to the sepulcher," said Joseph.

Ester peered through the door behind him. "Jesus will not be taken to your sepulcher on the backs of slaves."

"I am here to help."

"Then stay out of our way," Ester snapped. "We will carry him. Abatal. Tamar. Bring in the bier."

They squeezed past Joseph and went outside to commandeer the bier from the slaves.

Joseph's eyes widened with surprise. "This is . . . is highly irregular."

"Get used to it," Ester said. "You might be a believer, but you are not one of his followers. You're no true disciple."

"Well, I . . . I," Joseph stammered. "I . . . I couldn't have traveled the countryside amongst you."

"Get out of our way," Abatal commanded, forcing Joseph to sidestep clear of the entranceway. Abatal and Tamar entered the room carrying the bier.

"I can't believe you're still challenging me."

"That's because you still don't know who he was," Ester countered viciously. "You—you outsider, you, you member of the Sanhedrin, who chose to keep silent during the hour of his need, as Gath has fully testified."

"I've told you, she was not fully there! Enough!" Joseph ordered. "We've discussed this—"

"Not enough!" Ester's shocking rejection of Joseph's authority paralyzed everybody. "Secret disciple indeed. Secret while our Lord was in danger. Secret until the hour of his—" She looked at the shrouded figure. "His death."

Joseph stammered. "I've . . . I've told you that . . . that I claimed his body before . . . before Pilate himself."

"Yes. After it was safe," said Ester. "After he was already dead. Oh, how brave."

"I'm providing him with a fresh-cut sepulcher worthy of a King."

"King indeed." Ester sneered. "He served. He did not want to be served. Sepulcher indeed. The rich and the powerful are already altering who he is. It's begun. It's begun—"

"In his name—"

"No doubt. In his name."

"You twist my words," Joseph said nervously.

"You twist your own words, you, you interpreter of words." Ester grimaced. "I heard you admit to your brother Nicodemus that Pilate, brother Pilate, planned to bury him since he understood the politics of the approaching Passover's Sabbath." She noted Joseph's discomfort. "Yes, I overheard fragmented whispers between you two. You should be more careful. You forget that women and slaves, although invisible, have ears. We are present, damn you."

Joseph kneaded his temples. "All right. All right. It's true. Pilate was flirting with Herod and Caiaphas."

"Yes. Ugly. Ugly politics was shared between them. And you."

"Me!?"

Ester's exasperation was palpable. "Your counterfeit innocence makes me ill."

Joseph tried to justify his position. "Herod recognized Jesus as the King of Jews. Rome often honors their defeated foe, if the foe is a worthy King."

"Worthy of crucifixion?"

"Worthy of a burial."

Ester glanced at the surrounding women. "I see." Her expression hardened. "Twisted. Twisted. Men's logic."

Joseph's anger intensified. "It's true."

"You mean, it was politically safer for Pilate and Herod and Caiaphas and . . . and you!"

Joseph narrowed his glare. "Don't bark at me like a dog. I don't have to listen to this from . . . from—"

"A woman?" Ester laughed. "A creature lower than a canine bitch?" Ester's sisters were shocked by her viciousness.

Everybody was unraveling from the stress and strain of this horrible day. Men forgot how to believe. Women forgot how to obey. Children forgot how to play.

Joseph pressed his right hand against the doorjamb in an attempt to control his anger. "You women are taking this too far."

"That threat won't save you." Ester grimaced. The tension between them increased. "Where were you at the hour of his death? And where was your fellow Sanhedrin brother, Nicodemus?"

"Where *is* anybody?" He stepped toward Ester. "He and I will rebuke the Council of Seventy for condemning him—"

"Hail! All hail Joseph and Nicodemus! Hail Joseph who secretly honors our Messiah after his death."

Joseph's eyes widened with terror. "Don't you dare mock me!"

Ester ignored the threatening tone in his voice. "And hail Joseph of Arimathea who considers a menstruating woman too unclean to care for the dead. God. This will surely increase her uncleanliness for all time."

"All right. Perhaps it is about the blood. All right. I overheard you whisper to one of your sisters that you were . . . were—" Joseph scanned the room full of women, who were still paralyzed by the content of this argument between a powerful man and a power-less woman. "I suppose, that's what this argument is about."

Ester's eyes narrowed with disdain. "You will never know who he was. Blood? A matter of blood? Jesus would have loved the mixing of the blood. He loved to shake the Law." Her declaration shocked everybody in the room. She laughed. "How hard does he have to shake everybody around him before . . . before—" Ester exhaled in defeat. "We are not awak-ened. Rome has prevailed on this day."

Joseph was frightened. He frowned at Salome, who remained unresponsive, like her sisters. To his relief, Nicodemus entered the room; to his surprise, Ester challenged Nicodemus.

"What do you want?—you. You're no better than him."

Nicodemus' concerned expression flattened with confusion. "I . . . I heard the shouting. I . . . I heard arguing."

"You came here to defend him."

Nicodemus cringed. "I . . . I came to mediate. Yes."

"Agh. You men." Ester hissed. "He's a coward. And so are you."

"We're all afraid," Nicodemus whispered. "Who can dispute that?"

"Stop trying to hide behind your wealth."

"Joseph and I have it to give."

"Too late! You can't buy your way into the Kingdom of Heaven."

Joseph sought Nicodemus' attention by clearing his throat.

"He can't help you," Ester declared.

Nicodemus pointed an authoritative finger at Ester, "I can neither stop you from thinking what you believe to be true," then he smirked at Gath, "nor can I convince her that I opposed the Sanhedrin's verdict against Jesus."

"You didn't," said Gath, the old slave woman, who tended the charcoal fire in the courtyard complex next to Caiaphas' courthouse, where the Sanhedrin met and interrogated the arrested Jesus; the same charcoal fire that Peter stood near to warm himself as he denied their Master.

"Give it to him," said Ester.

"I heard everything," Gath insisted.

"Therefore, you think you know the truth." Nicodemus looked to Joseph for help.

"The truth is," Gath professed, "I heard a careful, quiet, coward abstain."

Everyone was shocked into a greater paralysis except for Ester, who drew power from Gath's fearless remark.

Gath pointed her bony finger at Joseph. "In fact, neither of them cast a true vote against the Sanhedrin's decision to condemn Jesus."

"How could we?" Joseph protested.

"That makes both of you careful, quiet, cowards who abstained," Ester charged. "And now, you're secret disciples who are trying to buy their way into the Kingdom of God, as well as trying to bribe us into offering both of you gratitude."

"That's not true," said Joseph.

"Wait, Joseph. Wait," Nicodemus muttered. "I'm not so sure about that."

"What are you saying?" Joseph was stunned by this sudden betrayal.

"I'm trying to say something . . . something close to the truth. The truth." Nicodemus pouted at Ester, then at Gath. "What is the truth?"

"Damn. Damn." The suddenness of Nicodemus' honesty dampened Ester's anger. "The truth is . . . is . . ." She stared at the shrouded figure on the bier. "We are here, and in love with the same man, and we are all weak, and . . . and he would have forgiven us all even if he had been angry with us and . . . and I don't know what is true?"

Guilt; regret; lost opportunity; shame; sorrow: the rubble of exhausted emotions was all there was left among them.

"We took him down from the cross and brought him here," Hanna said. Hers was the first gentle voice uttered since the beginning of this terrible confrontation. "Now we will take him to your—his sepulcher."

Joseph stammered. "But . . . but—"

"Take us to this sacred place," Ester commanded.

"Yes. Lead the way," said Abatal, who was prepared to help carry Jesus to this destination. The bier was still perched on the table beside her with her Lord's shrouded figure upon it.

Joseph of Arimathea bowed to these women of spirit. "All right, ladies. Night is approaching. Please. Let us proceed. Please. Let us make haste."

CHAPTER 14

Sorcery

Ester looked through one of the high windows in the main room and noted the strange gloom in the sky. "The celestial bodies seem confused. The sun and the moon and the stars seem to be at odds with each other."

"Yes. Odd," said Hanna. "Day into night. The heavenly forces of the light and the darkness seem to be reaching into the edge of each other's sky."

"And the four winds seem . . . seem to have carried away his spirit." Gath cupped her hand by her right ear. "Listen. Stay alert." Her eyes intensified. "Watch for his spirit to descend upon us."

"Old woman, please," said Joseph. "Please. Don't

add any sorcery to this approaching night. Please. Let's go before the real night descends upon us."

"He's right," said Ester, who lifted the head of the bier off the table with Tamar's assistance, which encouraged Abatal and Salome to lift up the other end. Together, they carried Jesus into the courtyard.

The sky threatened more rain. The stillborn glimmer that was left in this day was about to be extinguished by the approaching Sabbath night.

As soon as they were on the road leading to their final destination, Abatal caught sight of a distant silhouette. "Who is that?"

Salome sighed. "That's John."

"That poor madman," said Gath. "I think he's lost more of himself than your husband, Mara."

"I plan to find out," said Mara. "So help me God, I plan to find out who he is."

Gath sought John's silhouette. "He's gone."

"No more than a glimpse," said Ester. "It's just as well."

A thick rain began to fall in tiny droplets so densely packed that it muffled all the sound in the world.

"What is this?" Ester remarked, with bewilderment.

The strangeness of the inclement weather rattled the hard-won peace among them.

"Calm yourself, sister."

"Tamar's right," said Salome. "This procession is another test."

"He's with us, I think. Somehow, he is still with

us." Tamar's straightforward declaration spread quickly, in a whisper, among those in the procession:

"Within his shadow."

"He is with us."

"Another test."

"Our Jesus—"

"Walks in the shadows—"

"Still—"

"Still with us."

Everyone contributed utterances except for Blessed Mother, Blessed Sister, and Mary of Magdala; they led the procession by following it in silence.

CHAPTER 15

Tomb

The tomb's entranceway was cut into a rock-face located near a garden not far from Golgotha.

A circular stone, which was rolled aside to uncover three quarters of the entrance into the sepulcher, was ready to be moved back over the opening to seal the vault once Jesus had been placed inside. The sepulcher's exterior was so unpretentious, that it was possible to walk past the entrance without being aware of its presence.

"I'm glad this is not a cave," Ester mumbled, as the procession approached a flight of stairs, which led down to the entrance. She tightened her grip around her corner of the bier. Jesus had grown heavier.

Tamar shifted the weight on her side in response. The head of the bier bobbed momentarily. "For the rich, there's comfort even in death. Newly quarried, one of them said. Expensive."

"Those two can afford their bribe for atonement." Ester peered at Joseph and Nicodemus. "They're ignoring us."

"Who can blame them?"

"They deserved my wrath."

"True. But they've been suffering as well," Tamar whispered.

"At a safe distance. And in comfort." Ester could not conceal her resentment.

Because the entranceway was partially blocked by the stone disc, the procession was forced to squeeze past the opening at the bottom of the stairs. The height of the entranceway also forced them to stoop forward to gain entrance into the first chamber.

The tomb was dry and clean and dark; oil lamps were required to see.

The entrance into the second chamber was shorter and narrower, and required more agility and care to transport Jesus' body across its threshold. Once inside, they placed Jesus on a shelf within a niche that had been hand-hewn from the soft limestone wall, in the same way the double chambers of the sepulcher had been hewn from the limestone rock-face.

There was only one burial niche cut horizontally into one of the walls.

Odd, very odd, Ester thought. And grand. Very

grand of Joseph of Arimathea to have offered such a wealthy space to the Messiah.

Numerous women crowded into the inner and outer chamber.

Because of the magnitude of Jesus' death and the contrasting closeness of the chambers, grief was whispered with more breathiness than volume, and wailing was expressed from the heart without performance. Even though there were no professional mourners present, a harmonious mixture of despair arose beautifully from these women, particularly from the tight semicircle of mourners nearest Jesus' mother.

The beating of breasts to accent their anguish was subdued. There were no litanies.

Who would lead? Who would respond? Who knew what there was to petition?

Only his mother. Only his mother. And she remained silent.

There was no extreme drama. No rending of garments. No noticeable jostling for better positions. No tearing at their hair. In fact, the gentle and unprofessional mourning that characterized this orderly and ritually proper ceremony had an ordinary quality that calmed, even consoled, many of those present.

"I heard that John is standing in the garden outside," Gath carefully whispered to Hanna.

"And I heard he's been invited to join his mother," Hanna muttered, through the mantle that concealed her mouth.

"Both mothers, I heard. But he refused."

"You mean, he did not respond."

"Hmm. Same thing." Gath glanced in Jesus' direction. So many women were packed into the ill-lighted inner chamber, it was hard to see anything but the backs of mourners. "I think our Master has misjudged John."

"Be careful," Hanna whispered. "That . . . that can't be possible. Nobody here, especially Blessed Mother, can believe that."

"You mean, won't."

Hanna beat her breast gently in response. "Oh, God."

"Remember, our Jesus was still a man."

"Why are you stating the obvious? Are you afraid?"

"I'm . . . I'm not the only one claiming the obvious," Gath countered defensively.

"God in heaven," Hanna murmured. "I should have remained outside."

"Are you all right, my child?"

"Pressure." Hanna placed the palm of her left hand against the underside of her swollen abdomen. "My baby. I feel pressure. I need to go."

"You'll not get past this tight knot of women. You'll have to relieve yourself here."

"God."

The smell of wet wool and damp sorrow were mixed with the soot from the meager flames of the oil lamps that dotted the gloomy interior of the dark and cold tomb.

Such an environment could not have been compared to the darkness of a womb; that safe darkness, which could have only been imagined by these women—all of whom instinctively knew without having to know, that this present cold darkness of death was the opposite to the warm darkness before birth.

The faint odor of urine arose within the chamber.

Blessed Mother sat on the limestone shelf beside her son, and placed the palms of her hands together to pray. The aloe and myrrh impregnated linen that bound his body, as well as the impregnated shroud that covered his body, gave off a heavy scent of perfume. Blessed Mother's straightened back was an elegant example of public mourning.

The light of the oil lamps created deep shadows that shimmered from the flickering of these numerous flames, which were held as carefully as possible. Within this dark earth, these women held their breaths like babies inside their wombs.

"God bless Jesus," Abatal whispered.

"Our Master needs blessing?" Ephah inquired.

"Everything needs blessing."

"Hmm."

"Isn't that what we ask for when we pray?"

"I . . . I don't know."

Abatal stooped closer to Ephah's left ear. "And he encouraged both men and women to pray together. Imagine that kind of blessing."

"Revolutionary."

"This equal blessing, this freedom for women is so revolutionary that it has caused problems among our men." Abatal exhaled to convey her cynicism. "Men. Why are they afraid of us? What are they afraid of?"

"Boy-men, most of them."

"Jesus pointed to a future where women would no longer be restricted to the silence of . . . of your *'court of women,'* for instance."

"The temple will always be a man's domain," Ephah qualified. "Your Samaritan men are no different."

"Then . . . then within your women's section in the synagogue, during the reading of the Torah or during the recitation of the prayers, this silence will be challenged."

"Not in our lifetime," Ephah muttered.

"Then I may as well remain a Samaritan. And you—you must not have understood our Master during these past few months to have so little hope."

"Don't be so naïve."

"Didn't the power of our public prayers with him and his brother disciples have any impact on you? God was there, woman. God was with us."

"If you say so."

"My God, if you don't know, what are you doing here?"

Ephah inhaled to control her cynicism. "Please."

The uneasy silence that grew between them did not develop into resentment. They were tired and in true mourning for the man they both loved through their own reason, and through their own understanding of Jesus—their Master and their Lord.

The hierarchy of women survived even the interior of the sepulcher.

Blessed Mother sat by her son with Blessed Sister and Mary of Magdala flanking her left and right side.

Merab and Shelomith had merged with Susanna, Joanna, Mary, and Martha ever since Mara and Hanna and Salome had been demoted in status by their association with a Samaritan and an adulterer and with those who prepared Jesus' body for burial. Unclean. They were considered unclean even among women, and stood segregated even within Jesus' sepulcher. And now . . .

Some of the Daughters of Jerusalem and a few of the loyal Women of Galilee managed to pack themselves inside the two chambers of the tomb in an attempt to keep the chosen separated from the demoted. However, since the demoted and the other unclean anointers of Jesus' dead body were also his bier attendants, they were able to form into a tightly packed group within the inner chamber close to his body, as well as close to his high-strung feminine relatives and friends.

Blessed Mother brought her right hand to her mouth when she coughed, and startled Blessed Sister and Mary of Magdala. The surrounding women were aroused like an agitated flock of birds on the ground.

As soon as the flock settled, Blessed Sister led them into public prayer.

CHAPTER 16

Squabbles

On the following day, Judean and Galilean women challenged their husbands, their adult sons, their brothers, their fathers—any able-bodied man who would have been capable of standing at the foot of Jesus' cross.

"Where were you?" was the prevailing question in many of the households across the lower end of Jerusalem and across the surrounding countryside.

Palestinian men, who were not used to being challenged by their women, blanched at the exposure of their cowardly behavior, as well as at the reduction of their power. Despite the attempt to reestablish their domestic tyranny, the women steadfastly rejected them.

This was not going to be, many women made clear. Things were not going to be the same at home. Never. Not after witnessing the ultimate sacrifice by a real man, who treated them with the kindness of equality and the courtesy of respect.

On this day, however, there was no kindness or courtesy extended to any woman who asked her man: Where were you during his darkest hour?

The occupying Roman legionnaires were confused, at first, by all these domestic disputes. Then amused. Everywhere in the city and in the countryside, domestic squabbles erupted.

A man smashed a clay bowl against a wall. "How dare you question me!"

"Don't think you're going push your weight around this home anymore. Not after yesterday!"

"Woman, I'm warning you!"

"Why don't you warn a legionnaire?! Ha! Big man."

A man punched a hole in the wall of his dwelling.

"What good did that do you?" his wife shouted.

The man studied his injured fist, then pointed at the damaged wall. "That was your face."

"Don't you dare threaten me!" she shrieked.

A boy entered his home through a back door that led from a courtyard. "Mother? Are you all right?"

"Yes, dear."

"Get out of here!" the man shouted.

The boy cowered but disobeyed the command. "I'm not leaving."

The man approached the boy. "What did you say?"

The boy's mother stepped between them. "You strike him and so help me God, I'll . . . I'll—"

"What." The man turned to her. "What are you going to do?"

The woman grimaced. "I helped to provide the water that bathed our Lord's body. I stood outside in the courtyard and felt privileged to receive the washbowls of water transformed by his blood. I felt privileged to discard, and clean, and refill them with fresh water."

The man wanted to apologize. The man wanted her forgiveness. The man wanted this argument to stop before it was too late. The man wanted it to be yesterday again, in order to have a second chance. The man wanted to speak softly to her, but he barked. "So what!"

"Even bastard slaves are above women in some households. But not yesterday. Or last night. Or today." She squinted. "I'm not your slave. The Messiah saw to that."

"Woman, you're pushing me too far!"

"I'll push you as far as I want."

The man grabbed the boy by the front of his tunic. "I told you to go outside!"

"Don't hurt him!" She approached the man with an uncontrollable rage that startled him.

He threw the boy on the ground, then threatened her with a violent gesture.

She maintained her defiant stance.

The man turned to the boy. "I'm sorry." He stepped toward her. "I'm sorry, damn it!" The man's eyes shifted from side to side like a trapped animal. "Jesus. Jesus. Where are you now?" The man retreated from her and the boy, then pushed open the front door of the dwelling and stumbled into the daylight like a drunk.

"Father?"

The mother gestured at her son to be silent. "No, dear. Let him go."

The boy stood up, approached his mother, and waited for her caress. The boy felt her tears against the side of his face when she wrapped her arms around him. The sound of her repressed sobs came shortly after.

This is what occurred the following day between husbands and wives who were either close or distant followers of the man they called Messiah.

Mary of Magdala witnessed several domestic encounters and was exhausted by her efforts at mediation. She conducted herself in the way she thought her love, her Jesus, would approach her sister disciples. She wanted to live up to her love's, her Lord's standards. "Dear, God. Give me strength to be greater than myself." She ran into Mara on the streets at dawn. In fact, it was the second daybreak following the third day of his execution. Mara appeared exhausted. "Mara. Mara. Not you and Peter as well."

"Me, especially," Mara confessed. "What else could I have done but challenge my husband, who had gained our Lord's greatest confidence. He among all of us should have had the strength to . . . to face—"

"Death? Is that what you wanted from him? To sacrifice himself?"

"I don't know." Mara began to cry. "I left him."

"Then go back to him." Mary caressed her. "I'm not sure what our men should have done. We who are invisible can speak bravely."

"No." Mara broke away from Mary's embrace. "I don't believe that. Our . . . our lives were also in jeopardy. They still are. I'll not be ashamed of our commitment. I'll not be ashamed of being a woman."

"About that, you're right, of course. And it's true that at every turn we doubt ourselves. At every opportunity we are willing to deceive ourselves."

"They make us do that."

"Perhaps. But we also do it to ourselves."

"They have the power. They have the power!"

Mary exhaled. "I don't have the strength for this, Mara."

"I'm sorry."

"This is not the time for it."

"I know, I know, I'm sorry."

"I've got to go."

"Please don't be angry with me. I could stand that from anyone else but you."

Mary hugged her, then kissed her on the cheek. "I'm going to his tomb."

"I'll join you."

"Alone. I want as few of us there as possible. Please."

Mara inhaled. "Yes. Yes. I understand. You realize, his mother and aunt may still be there."

"That's not likely. They're even too exhausted to be angry."

Mara felt hurt. "I'm sorry."

"Oh, dear. I didn't mean anything by that."

"But—"

"Please. Believe me, Mara. That was not a slight. I promise." Mary searched Mara's eyes. "Do you believe me? Do you?"

Mara nodded, reluctantly. "Yes. Yes."

"Good." She reached for Mara's right hand and patted the back of it. "Go back to where you're lodging. Tend to the children. Wait for your husband to return."

"If he does."

"He will. Then forgive him. God knows, he won't forgive himself."

Mara nodded more confidently as she held back her tears. "All right. All right." She grabbed Mary's hand. "Please. Be careful. There's no telling what kind of riffraff is still out there. There are too many shiftless men looking for trouble."

"Not at this hour of the morning. They'll still be sleeping off their wine. Don't worry. Their behavior is predictable. Go back to your lodging, Mara. Go."

They kissed, then parted. Both women feared what the future held. Both women prayed that the God of Abraham would accompany them.

CHAPTER 17

Resurrection

Mary of Magdala glowed as if she were immersed in light when she walked out of Jesus' opened sepulcher a second time on the second daybreak following the third day of his crucifixion. She discovered Joanna, the wife of Chuza and the manager of Herod's household, and Merab, the mother of Peter. They appeared frightened.

"We saw you from a distance," said Joanna.

"We saw you enter the tomb," Merab added. "We were too frightened to follow you inside."

Mary was still in a trance. She looked past them and caught sight of someone at the far edge of the garden scurrying away. "Who's that over there?"

"That's Mary, the mother of James. She set out to tell our sisters what's happened." Joanna noted the glow in Mary's eyes. "What has happened?"

"He's gone," said Mary.

Merab shrieked with terror.

Joanna brought both hands to her chest. "Are you sure?"

"His . . . his body is gone, I told you."

Merab simpered.

Joanna took a long and deep breath. "Lord."

"And I saw . . ."

Joanna gaped at Merab. "You're frightening us."

"And I was frightened as well, believe me." Mary was still recovering from her experience. "After that earthquake—you must have felt it."

"Of course, we did." said Joanna

"We did, we did."

Mary studied both women. "And I was also para-lyzed with fear after that young man shared—"

"A man?" Joanna interrupted. "A man?"

"Who shared a message."

"He was a messenger," Merab qualified.

"Yes. An angel," Mary said. Her sisters were shocked. "He gave off a bright light and wore a white robe."

Merab gently beat her breast with her right hand to ease her palpitations. "You're frightening me, Mary."

"You don't know fear. I was so terrified, I allowed him to escort me into the second chamber of the tomb where he said, *'Don't be alarmed. You must be look-*

210

ing for Jesus the Nazarene who was crucified. Why are you looking for the living among the dead? He is not here. He was raised. Look at the spot where they put him. You see? He was raised, just as he said. Look. Come closer. Look at the spot where he was lying. Don't be frightened.'"

"What did you do?" Joanna inquired with intense anticipation.

Mary glanced at both women, and unintentionally increased the dramatic effect. "*'Run,'* the angel said. *'He is going ahead of you to Galilee.'*"

"To Galilee?" Merab repeated.

Mary nodded her head. "*'There you will see him,'* he said. *'So, go and tell his disciples, including Peter, that he's going ahead of you to Galilee.'*"

"Back to Galilee," Merab repeated.

"And then what?" demanded Joanna. "Then what?"

"I've told you," said Mary. "He told me, *'There you will see him, just as he told you.'*"

"And?"

"And . . . and I ran. I ran as hard as I could out of the tomb and into . . . into," Mary pointed to the north, "into that direction. I ran like a mad woman until . . . until there he was. But I didn't know it."

Joanna glanced at Merab. "There who was?"

"At first, I . . . I didn't know him. I didn't. Not until he said, *'Ephphatha.'*" (Be opened.) Mary raised her hands to her ears. "His voice opened me up."

"To what?" Merab implored.

Mary peered at her as if Merab had become possessed. "To him. To him! And it frightened me so much that I . . . I threw myself on the ground before him. Then he said, *'Talitha cumi.'* (Little girl, arise.) I raised my head and saw his smile. *'Talitha cumi,'* he repeated, and I rose as the little girl he spoke to, ready to hug him. Then he said, *'Don't touch me because I have not yet gone back to the Father. But go to my brothers and tell them this: I'm going back to my Father and your Father—to my God and your God.'"* Mary seemed as if she were coming out of another trance. "And now, here I am. Reporting what's happened to my sisters, first. I have seen the Master!"

"Praise the Lord," said Merab.

"*'Talitha cumi. Ephphatha,'*" Joanna repeated.

"Yes. Yes. *'Little girl,'* he said. *'Little girl, arise,'* and . . . and, *'be opened,'*" Mary said, in a euphoric state.

"And then what?" Merab entreated.

Mary was startled when Merab touched her left arm. "I . . . I ran. I . . . ran again. But I could not find anybody. All this good news inside of me. All this experience. All of this . . . this, what I saw, what I heard—and nobody. Nobody!"

"Then what? What?" Joanna trembled.

"I ran back here," said Mary, "And went inside the tomb again and . . . and when I came out again, I saw you two and . . . and now I'm . . . I'm here with you. Thank, God."

"Yes," said Joanna. "Thank, God. You looked like a mad woman when we first saw you. A mad woman."

"Well I . . . I suppose I was. But as you can see, I'm no longer consumed by fear."

"But you are still consumed by light," said Merab.

"That's right." Joanna peered hard at Mary. "There's still fire in your eyes. What happened? Did anything happen during your second visit inside his tomb just now?"

But just as Mary was going to share with them what had happened to her this time, she saw John with Hanna's husband, Aaron, approaching them. "Look."

The men were squinting at the half-light of the early morning as if they'd just recently awakened. They appeared exhausted and humbled by the recent past.

"He's gone!" Mary exclaimed, before either man had a chance to greet her. "The anointed one is gone."

John struggled to speak for the first time. "Our . . . our Master? He's . . . he's gone?"

Aaron was astonished that John was finally able to speak. "Are you all right?"

"No." John coughed. The back of his throat was dry and still dormant. He knew he did not have to explain himself before Mary, or to the other two women who had witnessed his behavior on Golgotha. He knew they would not embarrass him any more than he was over his behavior at the foot of their Master's cross—at least, not while standing in public with Aaron, who may or may not have heard about his madness that day. But then again, Aaron was a man, and there had been no other men present at his cross that day—at least, no man who professed to be one of his disciples. Not one. Only half of one: him;

John; a disciple too strangled by fear to speak up in his Master's defense; a creature too pathetic to stand up straight like a man before his tortured Rabbi. Instead, he groveled and whimpered like a mangy dog that deserved to be beaten and kicked off Golgotha by a Roman legionnaire.

"So? So what happened?" Aaron demanded.

Mary ignored John's obvious internal difficulties. "I . . . I saw two heavenly messengers."

"Two?" Merab inquired. Joanna nudged her in order to deflect her away from her surprise and confusion concerning this apparent contradiction.

"Yes. Two," said Mary.

"There are two men. Inside," Aaron qualified.

"No," said Mary. "Two angels. There were two figures in dazzling white cloaks that appeared and stood beside me."

"You?" said Aaron incredulously. "Just now?"

"Yes."

Aaron started to enter the tomb.

"They're no longer in there."

Aaron was relieved that he didn't have to enter the tomb, especially by himself. "I see." He masked his fear. "But . . . but how come it was you, who . . . who saw angels. How could it have been . . . been you—"

"A woman? Is that it? Is that my fault?"

"Not—only."

"Ahh. Then you would not believe this story if it had come from, from let's say, Peter as well."

"I . . . I wouldn't say that."

"Peter's words would have more weight," John reasoned, not meaning to be disrespectful.

"And, I suppose," Aaron continued skeptically, "these angels spoke to you."

"Yes."

"Ahh, then they spoke to nobody," said Aaron.

John ignored Aaron's insult to Mary. "Where is his mother?"

"She and her sister and the others—"

"Yes, yes."

"Well." Mary folded her arms under her breasts. "Exhaustion finally got the better of them. They were offered a place to sleep and had to accept it. Poor dears."

John controlled his impatience. "Yes. Well. These . . . these angels. You say they spoke to you."

Mary glanced at Joanna and Merab to keep them quiet. "Yes."

"And?" John prompted.

"Well. I neglected to tell you that there was an earthquake as I approached the tomb the first time."

"Oh, brother."

"It's true," Joanna qualified.

"Quiet, Aaron." John's patience was beginning to run thin. He cleared his throat.

"But—"

"Not one more show of disrespect. She has been one of his disciples from the beginning. And you, you know nothing."

Aaron's embarrassment smoldered in his eyes. "I've given my home to his disciples."

"To your credit," said John. "No one doubts the quality of your hospitality, or your generosity."

Aaron turned to Mary. "I'm sorry. It's difficult to listen to a woman give testimony."

Mary uncrossed her arms and lowered them to her side. "I'm a witness."

"A witness, yes. A woman giving testimony concerning this matter. Well. It will be difficult for many—any of us, to take you seriously."

"Men." Mary shook her head, then peered at Merab, who was too frightened to speak.

Aaron shrugged his shoulders. "I'm only presenting the truth."

"Agh." Mary sighed. "What is the truth? What will the truth become?"

"What it must become," said John. "Despite you or me or . . . or—"

"You're probably right." Her grin conveyed a deep cynicism. "But I'll not remain silent."

"Then speak." The tone in John's voice was sincere but not hopeful.

"And many more women of this world will not remain silent."

"No matter," said Aaron. John tapped Aaron's left arm with his right forearm in order to silence him.

"I guess I'll have to be satisfied with that," said Mary.

"Don't listen to him," John implored. "Go on. Tell me what happened to you there. Please."

"Well. After the ground quit shaking, an angel appeared in front of this tomb."

"What did he look like?" Aaron asked, in an attempt to make amends for John's sake.

John misunderstood him. He gritted his teeth. "Quiet." He softened with Mary. "Please, go on."

Mary took a glimpse at her sisters, who seemed to be holding their breaths, before she went on with her testimony. "He rolled back the large stone and escorted me to the other angel, who was sitting at the head of our Master's place of rest. Waiting."

"For you, you think?" John asked, deferentially.

"I don't know."

"Then what happened?"

"Well, the angel who escorted me inside sat at the foot of our Master's place of rest and said, *'Woman, why are you crying?'*"

"Ahh, the plot thickens."

John ignored Aaron's snide remark. "Go on. You were crying."

"Yes. I didn't realize I was until he told me so, but . . . but—"

"What did you say?"

"*'They've taken my Master away,'* I said, *'and I don't know where they've put him.'*"

"Can you remember what the angel looked like?"

Mary searched her memory. "No. Not really."

"Hmm." Aaron shifted his weight to one foot to emphasize his disbelief.

"But he gave off an intense light. Greater than fire. And his clothes were as white as snow. I could not tell his age. I could not bear to look into his eyes. I—"

"No matter," said John. "What else did he say? He did continue to speak."

"Eloquently."

"And?"

"He said, *'Why are you looking for the living among the dead? He is not here. He was raised.'*"

"She's possessed!" Aaron exclaimed.

"Look for yourself, if you dare!" Mary hollered.

Aaron turned to John. "Look at that!"

"What do you expect? Now shut up!" said John. He calmly turned to Mary. "Go on, please. Try not to listen to him."

Mary composed herself. "He said, *'Remember what he told you while he was still in Galilee: the son of Adam is destined to be turned over to pagans, to be crucified, and on the third day to rise.'*"

"My God. Then what?"

"When he saw that I was convinced of what he told me," Mary said offhandedly, "he said, *'Hurry. Tell his disciples that he has risen from the dead.'*"

"Risen from the dead." John recalled his Master's prophecy. "And you're sure this is what this angel said?"

Mary glanced at the other two women, who had remained stone silent in order to keep control of their confusion. "How could I have possibly misunderstood that?"

"Of course. Did he say more?"

"*'Behold,'* he said, *'he is going before you into Galilee. There you will see him. Now, you have been foretold.'*"

"What did you do?" John muttered.

"I hurried. I ran from the tomb mixed with fear and joy and uncertainty. I ran until," Mary peered at the other two women, "until I ran into him on the road north of here."

"You what?"

"There he was, before me."

"Who?"

"Him. Our Master. Jesus himself."

"Impossible," said Aaron.

"Shut up," John snapped. He calmed himself before addressing Mary. "You saw him and—"

"At first, I thought he was a gardener when he asked me, *'Woman, why are you crying? Who is it you're looking for?'* Then I said, *'Please mister, if you've moved him, tell me where you've taken him so I can take him away.'* Then he said, *'Mary. Hello.'*" Mary exhaled. "Then I realized who it was and . . . and I shouted, *'My God!'* I recognized him. *'Rabbi!'* I wanted to come to him and take hold of his feet and pay him homage, but I simply dropped to my knees in tears. Then he said, *'Do not be afraid. Go tell my companions so they can leave for Galilee, where they will see me.'*"

Joanna and Merab were startled by the contradictions in Mary's testimony, but they kept silent.

"And then what?"

"I rose to my feet because I wanted to come up to him. But he said, *'Don't touch me. I have not gone back to the Father. But go to my brothers and tell them this: I'm going back to my Father and your*

Father—to my God and your God!' " Mary shook herself out of another trance. "And now, here I am. Reporting to you, and my sisters here, everything I saw and experienced."

"But where did he go?" John pressed.

"Away," said Mary. "He blessed me and then . . . then he walked away."

"To where?"

"I . . . I don't know."

"You mean, you just simply let him go?"

"What was I to do?" Mary implored. "You of all people know how he was."

"Yes, yes. How. How was he?"

"He . . . he was Jesus. Our Jesus. He'd give us instructions, and his blessings, then he'd go about his business. Jesus."

"Fantastic." John was truly bewildered. "You, of all people."

"Not so fantastic."

"Please. Don't take offense," he said.

"It's hard not to," she countered.

"You were truly his closest . . ."

"Disciple. Say it."

"Yes."

"God. Why is it so difficult for you men? He loved me. And I loved him. That cannot be taken away. Do you understand? You or . . . or Peter cannot take that away." Mary beheld Merab. "I'm sorry."

"My son." Merab bowed her head. "I'm afraid he'll try."

"I'm afraid he'll succeed," said Mary.

"For now," Merab agreed.

"For a time," John tried to qualify.

"For all time," Mary insisted.

John sighed. "Perhaps." He avoided Merab's eyes. "Yes." Then avoided Mary's eyes. "It's probably true."

"I'll say nothing about this," Aaron murmured.

"We know," said Mary. She studied John's drawn face. "We know. Even your pathetic silence at the cross will ring louder than all the women's voices in Palestine, combined."

John stepped away from her as if cold water had been splashed into his face. "I'm sorry." He avoided Aaron's probing eyes.

"No you're not. You're a man. All you care about is your pride and honor among men. Go on. Go to your Peter. Seek your honor. Build your false pride."

Aaron attempted to pull John away from this crazy woman.

Mary was amused. "Go on. Pull him to safety. Push us aside. But I'll not be vanquished. Mary of Magdala. I will not disappear from his voice: Jesus. Jesus." Her laughter alarmed both men.

John broke Aaron's hold from his arm, then shot a hard glance at him. Aaron knew enough to let his senior take charge. Aaron lowered his gaze to convey his submission, despite the irregularity of this woman's behavior.

John could not end it here. He felt compelled to pursue the underlying meaning of her rebellion toward him. His cowardice alone was not the only reason. He shifted away from Aaron and searched uneasily for the correct delivery to the question he had in mind. "Sister. Peter knows that Jesus loved you more than any other disciple. Please. Tell me . . . tell me one of his secret thoughts. Something. Anything. Anything Jesus said to you and nobody else. Will you do that for me?"

"For what purpose?" Mary asked.

"Good point," Aaron agreed. "For what purpose?"

"Quiet, Aaron. You know nothing." John composed himself. "Listen to what the woman has to say." He nodded to Mary. "Please. Tell me. I would like to share this with Peter someday."

Mary chuckled. "Good luck."

"I swear. I'll wait until he is ready. I'll wait until I know Peter is listening."

"His name was not given to him by our Master for the wrong reason," Merab interjected. "Believe me, I know. I'm Simon's mother."

John chuckled. "Yes. Yes. The Rock." He pursed his lips, then waited.

"All right," Mary said, thoughtfully. "One day. One day I told Jesus that I saw him in a vision. He congratulated me for not wavering at seeing him, and then he said, *'For where the mind is, there is the treasure.'* So I said, 'My Lord, how does someone who has a vision see it? Through the soul or through the spirit?' And he answered, *'The seer doesn't see with either. The visionary sees with the mind which lies between the soul and the spirit.'*" Then Mary fell silent and awaited John's rejection.

Aaron felt the heavy silence between them and

was confused by it. He waited for John to show him the correct response to this strange atmosphere created by Mary's declaration of intimacy between her and the Messiah; John ignored him. "Are you accepting that our Lord spoke secretly to her and not to . . . to you or . . . or Peter? Surely it's not possible that Jesus gave the impression that she was more worthy of his intimacy than a man."

Mary of Magdala lost her temper. "How dare you! You, who have only recently joined us." She glared at John. "And you. John, my brother. John. How do you respond to this? You must know me well enough by now to know that I would never invent the things shared to me by him. I would never tell lies about our Master!"

John could not look directly into Mary's eyes. "I'm sorry. Aaron here is a lot like Peter. Their inclinations toward anger and envy and suspicion are constant emotions, which they are always ready to give way to."

"I can surely testify to that concerning my son," said Merab.

Aaron directed his heat toward Merab. "And what man could not doubt a woman for insinuating that she was better than him by knowing Jesus more intimately?"

"Damn it! Shut up, Aaron! Or so help me God I'll . . . I'll . . ." John controlled his anger. "See? Even now you're showing your envy by questioning this woman as if she was your adversary."

"Like Peter—"

"Precisely!"

Aaron cupped his mouth with the palm of his right hand as if trying to contain the ugliness that he had been accused of.

"Peter will perform no better," Mary scorned.

"If our Lord considered you to be worthy," said John, "who is Peter to disregard that?"

"Do you really believe that?"

"I . . . I want to, Mary. I know that Jesus knew you completely and . . . and loved you devotedly. It's not possible to have traveled together and not perceived that. Not possible."

"Well then?" Mary waited hopefully.

"I don't know how I'll be able to convey your good news to the others," said John.

"You mean, to Peter."

"Yes, well—he's rarely alone."

"Then you mean, to the other men," said Mary.

"Yes. Disciples."

"You're excluding the women?" Mary's exasperation increased. "Their discipleship has great meaning as well."

"I'll leave that up to you."

"I see." Mary lost all hope. "Then it truly has begun."

"What has?"

"The separation between us that Jesus never intended for us to develop."

"Men are men. Women are women."

"And without him, we are no longer equal."

"I think that was an illusion."

"I see." Mary sniffed. "His vision is already dissipating." She turned away from John and began walking.

"Where are you going?"

Mary ignored him.

"Where are you going?" John cried out a second time.

"Where. Does it matter?" Mary stopped walking, but kept her back to him and Aaron. "I'm already invisible."

The men took the opportunity to hustle away from Mary as the women ran toward her.

"Why the differences in your story between us and them?" Joanna solicited.

"There were no differences. It's what happened. How I felt. All of it. Besides, they're men. Men require larger visions. They didn't trust in anything I said anyway."

"True. True." Joanna squinted. "But . . . but you did speak the truth to us, didn't you?"

"Of course."

"And John . . . John, he did defend you from Aaron," Joanna said reassuringly. "He did seem convinced."

"For now," said Mary.

"Peter's influence will change that," said Merab. "I'm sorry. I know my son."

"And I knew Jesus. He was mine. You both know that. And I was his."

"And they are jealous," added Joanna.

"Especially my Peter," said Merab, the mother of

Simon-Peter. She felt insecure with the burden of her son's flaws.

Joanna took Merab by the hand to express her sympathy, then peered at Mary. "You spoke the truth. Didn't you?"

"Yes," said Mary of Magdala. "But the truth will not be heard."

Merab squeezed Joanna's hand. "Men."

CHAPTER 18

Peter

John was angry: with himself, with Aaron, with Rome.

Aaron was perplexed: with John, with Mary, with his wife, Hanna. He knew it was prudent to remain quiet during their hunt for Peter, and equally prudent to remain a spectator, when they found him, long enough to see how they behaved with each other.

Somebody shouted.

"Hold it," said John. "That sounds like him."

Aaron saw a figure lying on his side with his back against a wall in an alleyway. "Over there. Is that him?"

"I'm not sure."

As they approached the man, he sat up and straightened his legs. He winced, then shouted at heaven. "I'm forgiven! Jesus! He's forgiven me! I know it!"

Aaron pinched his nose. "Is that him?"

"Yes. He's talking in his sleep, I think."

"Is that what you call it? He reeks of wine and vomit. He appears delirious to me."

"Careful," said John. "Address him carefully. He can be unpredictable."

"From what I see, you don't need to convince me. You speak to him first."

"Peter? Peter." John crouched near him. Peter smelled bad. "What's happened to you?"

Peter squinted at John, then at Aaron. He rubbed his eyes with the back of his hands in an effort to understand who he was seeing.

"Peter, it's me."

"John? Is that you?"

Aaron crouched beside John.

"Where have you been?" John asked. "We've been looking all over for you."

"I . . . I was at . . . at . . ."

"My place for a time," said Aaron.

Peter studied the unfamiliar man. "Your place? Who are you?"

"I'm Aaron. You helped fix my wall, remember?"

"What wall? Ahh. Yes. Your wall, yes."

"You left his home before we were able to get back," John added. "We just missed you, I think."

"You missed me by far more than that," said Peter. "Where have you been?"

"Looking for you," said John. "And everybody else. Scattered. We're all so scattered."

Peter licked his lips. "I saw him."

Aaron and John exchanged furtive glances.

"Saw? Saw who?" John coaxed.

"Our Master. He's alive. I swear. I saw him."

John licked the left corner of his dry mouth. "Are . . . are you sure?"

"Don't look at me like I'm crazy."

"I'm not. I assure you. I . . . I—you tell him, Aaron."

Peter looked at Aaron, who shifted his weight onto his knees. "Tell me what?"

"Thaddaeus saw him as well," Aaron said.

"From a distance," John qualified.

"Just as he was awakening," Aaron further stipulated. "But saw him nonetheless."

"But that's not all," John added.

"What?"

"There were others—"

"Who saw him?"

"Yes." John peered at Aaron for support.

"Well?" Peter pressed his back against the alley wall. "Who?"

"It . . . it was Mary of Magdala and . . . and your own mother who saw that our Lord had risen."

"At his tomb? My . . . my own mother as well?"

"So it seems," said John.

"And at the foot of his cross. They were—" Peter rubbed his dry, cracked lips with the back of his left hand. "My mother is certainly not one for idle tales."

"And neither is Mary."

Peter's face twitched. "Yes. No. But why—I mean—they, our women, of all people, have seen him when . . . when . . ." Peter suppressed the disconcerted tone in his voice and remained quietly harassed for a long time. "My view of him was not from a distance," he said emphatically. His eyes shifted guardedly from John to Aaron and back. "I touched him." Their response was not sufficient to dispel his insecurity. "I touched him, I said!" Peter crossed his arms over his chest and rocked from side to side. "Women," he muttered. His eyes betrayed his jealousy. "The two of you are not toying with me, are you?" His eyes darkened. "If you're toying with me, I swear—"

"I wouldn't do that," said John. "You should know by now that my humor is not of that kind."

Peter leaned forward and rested his forearms against the thighs of his crossed legs. He was emotionally exhausted. He released a long sigh followed by a long convulsive sob. When he finally gazed at John and Aaron, his eyes were shining. "He's risen from the dead. He's returned, like he said he would. And I saw him. *I* felt the cold wound to one of his wrists. I . . . *I.*"

John peered uneasily at Aaron before he sat beside Peter. "Tell us more about what happened?"

Peter shrugged his shoulders. "He appeared twice. I touched him once. We spoke both times."

"Of what?"

Peter squirmed, then pressed his back against the

wall. "He asked me, *'Do you love me more than these?'*"

"These what?"

Embarrassed, Peter answered, "I don't know. I was too overjoyed to ask and too afraid to break the spell of my vision. I was grateful to hear his—"

"Yes, yes, our Master hasn't changed his manner. But what did you say?"

"Yes," said Aaron. "Did you answer him?"

"Of course!"

"And!"

"I said, *'You know that I love you.'*"

"Good." Aaron nodded. "Good answer."

John gazed at Aaron and pressed his right forefinger against his lips in a gesture for silence. "Peter. Continue."

Peter searched his memory. "Well, I . . . I don't want to sound self-serving."

"It's too late for that now," said John. "I don't care about any of that. Just tell me what the two of you said."

Peter took a deep breath. "*'Take care of my lambs,'* he said. Then, then he called me Simon for the second time. *'Simon, son of John.'*"

"And why not Peter?" John queried with intense curiosity.

"I . . . I don't know. I wanted to ask him but . . . but—"

"What?"

"He . . . he asked me if I loved him, again. So, my thoughts naturally turned away from myself."

"And?"

"I said, *'Yes, Lord, you know I love you.'* Then he said, *'Take care of my sheep.'* And harassed me a third time with the same question."

"The exact one?"

"Yes: *'Simon, son of John, do you love me?'*" Peter was disturbed and sad and bewildered. He searched John's and Aaron's eyes. "I'm nothing, I know that now."

"Yes, yes, but what did you say?"

"What else could I say but, *'Lord, you know everything; you know that I love you!'*"

John shook his head. "Peter, Peter, will you never stop yelling at him?"

"No. No! You don't understand. I was shouting, yes. But at myself. Myself! Because . . . because . . ."

"Don't stop there," said Aaron.

"Because I believe he's forgiven me for my denials."

"Ah." John understood. "Mara told us about your denials."

"Yes. Mara." Peter nodded bitterly. "She left me." He noticed their confusion. "No matter. That's another matter." He became irritated by their persistent confusion. "She doesn't matter!" He drew a deep breath. "Never mind. Yes. There were three denials before the cock crowed: as he predicted. Three denials. Followed by three tests and three charges."

"From your vision," Aaron qualified.

"No. Not a vision. No." His eyes blazed with confirmation. "He was real. I know it." Peter sat up more confidently. "His three questions about my love were his sign of forgiveness, don't you see? He not only forgave me for each of my denials, he told me to follow him, to take care of his lambs." He wiped his nose with the back of his forearm. "And I will, I swear. I'll follow him to the bitter end, I swear, I'll—"

"Easy, Peter." John pressed his right hand against Peter's shoulder.

"But . . . but what is our mission without his guidance?" Aaron asked cautiously. He threw a puzzled glance at John. "Where is his kingdom? What do we do now?"

"We're going to sit steadily and wait," John answered with great determination. "Another sign will come. More of his message will reach us." The tone in his voice was too fervent. "I know it. I know it!"

"Patience," Aaron muttered. "He will come again—I hope."

Peter stirred restlessly. "I may have been forgiven—even invited, again, to follow him. But I . . . I don't know enough, feel worthy enough to be an apostle. For God's sake just . . . just look at us. We're a shabby lot. That's right: worn and threadbare, petty and mean."

"Don't speak that way," John pleaded.

"Sure, sure, easy for you to say. He loved you best."

"He loved us all!"

"But you. Always you he confided with—"

"And Judas and you—"

"He always challenged! Not confided. Me? Bah!"

John grimaced after licking the acidity from his lips. "You were almost second in command."

"Almost," Peter said resentfully.

"That's right. If you'd been smart enough to lead."

"Easy, there," cautioned Aaron. "I don't understand what this is about between you. But, well, look at him. He's still not recovered from his drunken fever." To Peter: "Don't take John seriously."

"I'm recovered. This leftover reek of wine you smell is not affecting me. I'm recovered!" The other two held their breaths. "But to what? To this pitiful congregation of frightened and confused idiots?"

"You seem to have placed yourself on a lofty level of judgment."

"Oh no, John. I'm describing myself, as well. In fact, I'm the lead idiot—no longer almost second in command." Peter gestured at his general condition. "See? Look at my depraved appearance. What kind of fool do I look like?"

"A frightened one," Aaron said. "You're right. And a confused one, like the rest of us idiots." His clownish method of delivery brought a smile to John's and Peter's faces; a cascade of verbal eagerness followed:

"We are lost—"

"And yet, we are bound."

"To become—"

"His apostles—"

"Of course!"

"And bound—"

"To him, even after death—"

"Which no longer exists—"

"Because of his death?"

"No. Because of his life. His resurrection. He was flesh, I tell you. He was flesh! I touched him. And I know."

"Then what shall we do next?"

"Wait. That's what we're bound to do."

"Because that's all there's left to do."

"Is this part of the faith, my brothers?"

"No. No. It's all of it." Peter leapt to his feet with excitement. "And he's bound to show himself to me, again."

"You think so?"

Without notice or invitation, Peter started walking toward the nearby crowded street of the city. It had stopped raining.

"Where are you going?" John asked.

"To offer my humble prayers at the tomb of his resurrection."

"Yes! Good. But . . . but then what?"

"Then . . . then it's time to go back to fishing."

John stroked his bright red beard in dismay. "We haven't cast our nets in years."

"We have to eat." Peter turned to them. "So, I'll cast my nets until . . . until, well, until I hear his next call."

"Ah. Yes. *'Follow me,'*" John whispered, in remembrance of the first call.

"Yes. *'Follow me.'*" Peter's voice was clear and steady. "Which one of us could ever forget the power of his *follow me?*" He turned away from them and began walking again.

"But wait!" Aaron shouted.

"Yes, wait for us!"

"I can't," said Peter. "I can no longer wait without the belief in his presence."

And John followed him as he'd never followed him before. And they followed him to seek the one who had been made flesh, once again, as it had been promised them in order for them to follow—or so they thought or heard or saw in their visions and their hope for the future of man, and woman, and . . .

About the Author

D. S. Lliteras is the author of eight critically acclaimed novels and one book of haiku and photography. He resides in Virginia Beach, Virginia, with his wife, Kathleen.

Hampton Roads Publishing Company

. . . for the evolving human spirit

Hampton Roads Publishing Company
publishes books on a variety of subjects,
including metaphysics, health,
visionary fiction, and other related topics.

For a copy of our latest catalog, call toll-free
(800) 766-8009, or send your name and address to:

Hampton Roads Publishing Company, Inc.
1125 Stoney Ridge Road
Charlottesville, VA 22902

e-mail: hrpc@hrpub.com
www.hrpub.com